WHERE THINGS COME FROM

AND HOW THINGS ARE MADE

Contents

WHERE FOOD COMES FROM

Janet Cook and Shirley Bond S.R.D.

Designed by Chris Scollen
Illustrated by Teri Gower and Guy Smith
Editorial assistance from Felicity Brooks

Contents

About food

You need lots of different types of food to keep you strong, fit and healthy. This book explains where each type of food comes from and what happens to it before it reaches your plate.

The story of food

Long ago, people spent most of their time searching for seeds and berries to eat.

They also hunted animals. Often they could not find any food and they had to go hungry.

Later they discovered how to tame animals. They protected them from wolves, then killed them when they needed food.

After a while, they found out how to grow plants by sprinkling seeds on the ground. They then ate these plants.

Famines

Some parts of the world, for example North Africa, have poor soil and hardly any rain. In a very dry year little grows. People have no money to buy food from elsewhere.

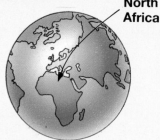

North Africa

Sometimes they have to eat seeds which should be planted for the following year. The next year they starve. This is called a famine.

They now had all their food around them in one place. Because of this, people were much less likely to go hungry.

Swapping food

Some food can only grow in a particular climate. For example, grapes need plenty of warm sun, and rice needs lots of rain.

Many kinds of food are sent abroad. This means people in cool places can buy grapes and people in dry places can buy rice.

Goods going into a country are called imports. Goods sent out of a country are called exports.

Rain dances

American Indians used to believe that rain was sent by rain gods. They tried to please these gods by dancing for them. They hoped this would make the gods send rain to help their crops grow.

Preserving food

Fresh food can soon go bad. Because of this, food is treated so it lasts longer and is safe to eat.

Freezing
Frozen food will keep for many months in a freezer.

Pickling
Some foods are put in jars of vinegar.

Canning
Food is put into clean tins which are sealed and heated.

Drying
Some foods, such as fruit and wheat, can be dried in the sun.

Pickled eggs

Frozen peas

Frozen fish

Dried apple rings

Pickled onions

Oats

Baked beans

Dried figs

Tomatoes

Wheat

Bread

Have you noticed how many different sorts of bread there are? Here are just a few of them.

Bread is made mostly of flour. The colour and taste depends on what type of flour the baker uses.

What is flour?

Most flour comes from a type of grass known as wheat*. The seeds or grains are removed and crushed to make flour.

Wheat

Grain

Split loaf

Chollah

Cottage loaf

Bloomer

Pitta bread

Sandwich loaf

Soda bread

Rolls

Chapatti

Baps

Naan bread

Rye bread

French stick

What happens at the bakery?

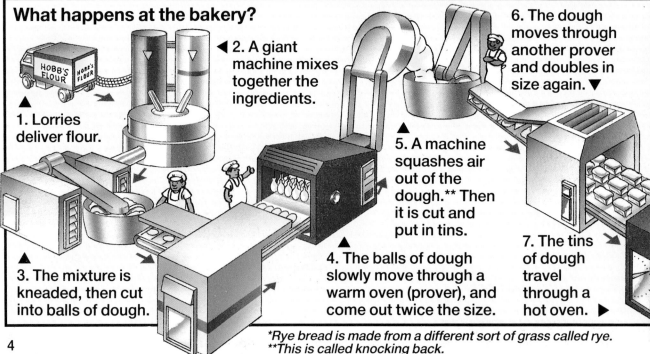

1. Lorries deliver flour.

◀ 2. A giant machine mixes together the ingredients.

3. The mixture is kneaded, then cut into balls of dough.

4. The balls of dough slowly move through a warm oven (prover), and come out twice the size.

5. A machine squashes air out of the dough.** Then it is cut and put in tins.

6. The dough moves through another prover and doubles in size again. ▼

7. The tins of dough travel through a hot oven. ▶

4

*Rye bread is made from a different sort of grass called rye.
**This is called knocking back.

Make your own bread

Home-made bread tastes delicious.

You will need:

200g strong white flour
200g wholemeal flour
2 teaspoons sugar
1.5 teaspoons salt
15g lard
15g fresh yeast
250 ml warm water

1. Mix the yeast and water. Now mix everything to make dough.

2. Fold the dough towards you then push it down and away.

Loaf tin

3. Turn it and repeat until it's no longer sticky. Put it in a tin.

4. Rub oil in a plastic bag. Put the tin in it. Leave in a warm place.

5. After an hour, remove from the bag and bake in a hot oven* for half an hour.

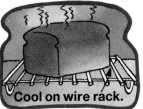

Cool on wire rack.

6. Remove from the tin. Does it sound hollow when tapped underneath?**

10. The bread ▶ is delivered to the shops.

9. Some are sliced and wrapped.

8. The loaves are tipped out of their tins and cooled on racks.

What makes bread rise?

If you make your own bread, you will see that the finished loaf is bigger than the dough you started with. The ingredient which makes dough grow (rise) is the yeast.

When it is warm, yeast gives off tiny bubbles of a gas called carbon dioxide. It is the bubbles that makes the dough rise.

Look at a slice of bread. Can you see tiny holes left by the carbon dioxide?

Flat bread

Some bread is made without yeast, and is quite flat. This is unleavened bread. There are four types shown on the opposite page; can you guess which ones? (Answer on page 74.)

*Gas mark 8, or 450°F, 230°C (electric).
**If it doesn't, put it back in the tin and leave for about five minutes longer.

Milk and eggs

Most milk comes from cows. A cow cannot give us milk until she has had her first calf. After that, she produces much more than a calf could drink; about 4,000 litres each year.

At the farm

◀ 1. On large dairy farms, the cows are milked by machines linked by pipes to enormous refrigerated tanks.

2. Each day, a refrigerated tanker collects the milk and takes it to the dairy. ▼

Tank

How cream is made

Warm milk is poured into a centrifuge. This machine separates the cream by spinning the milk very quickly.

A switch on the centrifuge controls how thick the cream is.

Very thin – single

Thin – whipping

Thick – double

Very thick – clotted

You can tell how thick cream is by its name.

JOE'S DAIRY

The milk flows from the tank to the lorry through this pipe.

The dairy has to be very clean and hygienic.

Tankers with milk from lots of farms in the area.

At the dairy

3. The milk is tested to make sure it is clean. Most milk is then heated for around 15 seconds, then quickly cooled down.

This is called pasteurising. It destroys any harmful germs in the milk and keeps it fresh for longer.

4. Machines pour the milk into cartons, bottles or cans. They are then loaded on to lorries and delivered to shops.

6

Make your own yoghurt

You will need:

750ml longlife milk

2 teaspoons fresh natural yoghurt

2-3 tablespoons dried skimmed milk

chopped fruit or nuts (optional)

1. Mix a little longlife milk and the yoghurt.

2. Stir in the remaining milk and the dried milk.

3. Cover with a tea-towel, and leave in a warm place.

4. After about 12 hours, add chopped fruit or nuts.

Crate of milk bottles

Milk lorry

Eggs

Most of the eggs you eat come from chickens. Sometimes the egg box tells you about the lives of the chickens that laid them.

★ Free range chickens roam around a farmyard, eating whatever they find. You have to hunt for the eggs.

★ Deep litter chickens live in a warm shed with straw on the floor. The farmer gives them special food.

★ Battery chickens are kept in cages and given special food. The eggs are collected from a tray below the cage.

From the farm to the box

Every day, large farms send eggs to a packing station. Here, workers measure them, then shine a bright light on them which shows if any are bad. They then pack them into boxes.

How fresh is your egg?

Place your egg in a glass bowl full of water. Now watch to see what it does.

Fresh	Not so fresh	Bad

There is an airspace inside one end of the egg. The older the egg, the larger the space, and the more likely it is to float.

7

Cheese and butter

Butter and cheese are both made from milk. Here you can find out how they are made. You can also discover why margarine was first invented.

The story of butter

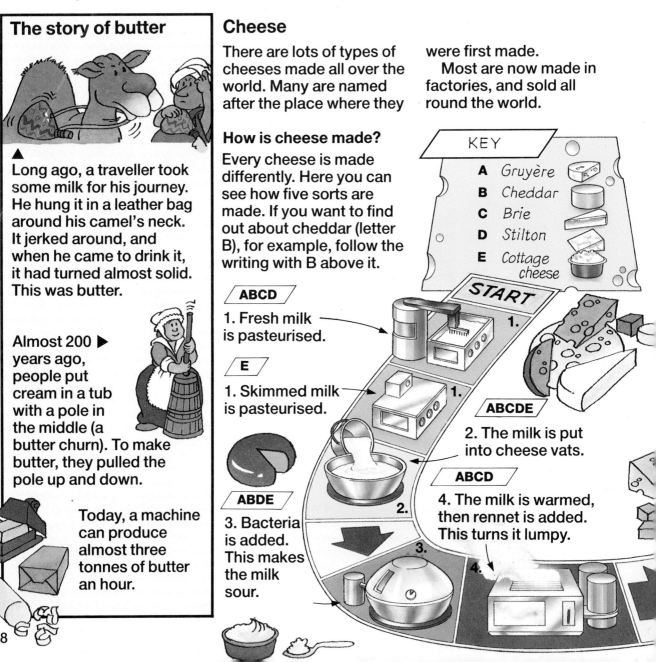

▲ Long ago, a traveller took some milk for his journey. He hung it in a leather bag around his camel's neck. It jerked around, and when he came to drink it, it had turned almost solid. This was butter.

Almost 200 ▶ years ago, people put cream in a tub with a pole in the middle (a butter churn). To make butter, they pulled the pole up and down.

Today, a machine can produce almost three tonnes of butter an hour.

Cheese

There are lots of types of cheeses made all over the world. Many are named after the place where they were first made.

Most are now made in factories, and sold all round the world.

How is cheese made?

Every cheese is made differently. Here you can see how five sorts are made. If you want to find out about cheddar (letter B), for example, follow the writing with B above it.

KEY

A Gruyère
B Cheddar
C Brie
D Stilton
E Cottage cheese

START

/ ABCD /
1. Fresh milk is pasteurised.

/ E /
1. Skimmed milk is pasteurised.

/ ABDE /
3. Bacteria is added. This makes the milk sour.

/ ABCDE /
2. The milk is put into cheese vats.

/ ABCD /
4. The milk is warmed, then rennet is added. This turns it lumpy.

8

Margarine

About 150 years ago, there was a shortage of butter in France. Hipolyte Mège Mouries invented margarine. It looked like butter but had a pearly shine.

The word margarine comes from the Greek margaritarion, meaning pearl.

Nowadays, most margarine is made from vegetable oil which is pumped with gas to make it go solid. Extra ingredients are then added to make it look like butter.

A
6. The lumps are cooked, pressed in moulds, then left in a cellar for six months. Here the cheese gives off bubbles. This makes holes in it.

B
6. The lumps are wrapped in cloth and pressed in moulds.

C
6. The lumps are left until the surface goes mouldy. This ripens the cheese from the outside inwards.

D
5. The liquid is drained away very slowly to leave moist lumps.

Brie has to be made flat so that the inside ripens quite quickly.

C
5. The milk is cut, so some of the liquid drains away.

ABE
5. The milk is cut, so the liquid drains away.

D
6. The lumps are left in ripening rooms. Here they are pierced with needles. This lets air in and makes it mouldy.

E
6. The lumps are washed, drained, and divided into small pieces.

FINISH

Fruit and vegetables

Some fruit and vegetables are grown in this country, but many are bought from countries which have a different climate.

They are all plants or parts of plants such as roots and stems.

You eat the centre of an artichoke, and the bottom of its petals.

These are the leaves of plants, picked before the flower comes out.

Celery

Asparagus

These are the bulbs of plants.

Lettuce
Endive
Spinach
Cabbage

These are the stems of plants.

Broccoli

Onion

Leek

Spring onion

Nuts

Most nuts are fruits or seeds that come from trees. Coconuts come from a type of palm tree.

This is what the inside of a coconut looks like.

Nuts

These vegetables are the flowers of plants.

Cauliflower

These are the roots or underground stems (tubers) of plants.

Tomato

These vegetables are the fruits of plants.

Courgette Carrot

Potato

Pulses

Dried beans, peas and lentils are called pulses. They must be soaked before being cooked.

Chick peas

Haricot beans

Red kidney beans

Chilli

Cucumber

Pepper

How bananas get here

Banana tree

Bananas grow in hot places like the West Indies. A large red flower comes out of the middle of the trunk. When this opens up there is a stem with about 100 bananas on it.

Sweetcorn is made into cornflakes, popcorn and a type of flour (cornflour).

10

*See page 3 for more about importing.

Apple

Orange

Lemon

Grapefruit

Grapes grow on a plant called a vine. Some are dried to make raisins. Some are made into wine.

These are called citrus fruits. They grow on trees.

Berries and soft fruit grow on bushes or plants.

Strawberry

Mango

Most mushrooms are grown especially for eating. Wild ones can look like poisonous toadstools, so don't pick them.

Avocado
Peach

Plum

Apples and pears can be eaten raw, but some are better cooked.

Cherry

Dates grow on palm trees.

These are stone fruit (they have a stone in the middle). They grow on trees.

Making crisps

Crisps are made from potatoes.

▲ First the potatoes are washed and peeled.

A machine ▶ slices them thinly. They are fried in hot oil, then drained and sprinkled with salt and flavourings.

◀ A machine weighs the crisps into bags.

▲ The bananas are picked when they are still hard and green.

On board ship, they are kept cool so they don't ripen too quickly.

◀ The stems are unloaded and taken to warm, damp rooms. When they are nearly ripe, they are cut into bunches called hands.

These are sent to fruit markets and shops all over ▼ the country.

TROPICO

11

Fish

Most fish are caught at sea in nets dangling from boats called fishing trawlers. The fish have to be rushed back to port very quickly, before they go bad.

Sometimes the fish are stored in freezers on the trawler instead.

Deep sea trawler

Open purse seine net

Catching fish

Deep sea trawlers catch fish from the bottom of the sea. They drag their nets along the sea-bed.

A trawler with a purse seine net catches fish which swim nearer the surface. Once the net is full, fishermen pull in the rope around the top of it.

The life of a salmon

When a salmon is about two years old it swims downstream towards the ocean.

After four years in the sea, it returns to its original river, using the sun to find its way. It knows its home by its smell.

The salmon leaps over anything in its path.

Most salmon then stay in the river until they die, but a few do the journey again.

Different sorts of fish

There are more than 30,000 different sorts of fish living in the seas, rivers, streams, lakes and ponds around the world. There are four main groups of fish: white fish, oily fish, freshwater fish and shellfish.

Oily fish, ▶ such as mackerel, mostly live in the sea.

Mackerel

White fish can ▶ be round (such as haddock), or flat (such as plaice).

Plaice

Freshwater fish, such as trout and salmon, mostly live in lakes and rivers.

Trout

Crabs ◀ Shellfish (such as crabs, prawns and mussels) mostly live on the sea-bed.

Mussels

Prawns

Preserving fish

Unless fish is eaten very soon after it is caught, it has to be treated to stop it from going bad. You can get food poisoning from bad fish.

Drying ▶

Long ago, people learnt to dry fish in the sun and wind.

Smoking ▶

Hanging fish over a fire preserves it and gives it a smokey flavour.

Freezing ▶

Fish lasts for up to three months in the freezer.

Salting ▶

Ancient Egyptians used salt to preserve fish.

Pickling ▶

Soaking fish in vinegar and salt is known as pickling.

How fish fingers are made

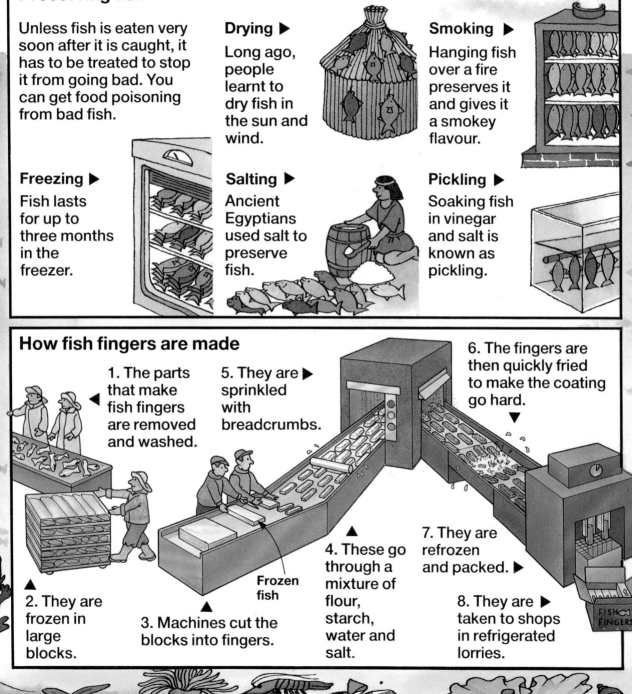

1. The parts that make fish fingers are removed and washed.

5. They are ▶ sprinkled with breadcrumbs.

6. The fingers are then quickly fried to make the coating go hard.

7. They are refrozen and packed. ▶

2. They are frozen in large blocks.

Frozen fish

3. Machines cut the blocks into fingers.

4. These go through a mixture of flour, starch, water and salt.

8. They are ▶ taken to shops in refrigerated lorries.

Meat

People have always killed animals for food. Cavemen spent their days hunting animals, and in some places there are still tribes of people who hunt animals.

Most of the meat we eat nowadays comes from farm animals.

Red and white meat

There are two main types of meat; red meat and white meat. Beef, lamb and pork are all red meat.

White meat comes from birds such as chickens, turkeys and ducks.

◀ Beef comes from cows. Most cows are killed when they are between the age of one and two. Meat from a young calf is called veal.

Pork and bacon both ▲ come from pigs. Pigs are killed when they are the right weight.

Lambs are usually killed ▲ when they are a year old. After this, the meat is called hoggett or mutton.

Chicken

Duck

Turkey

From the farmer to your plate

Here you can see what happens to the animals before they get to your plate.

Farmer

Cows and sheep mainly eat grass. In the winter, other crops such as hay and barley are also given to them.

Pigs like lots of different foods. Famers give them a special mixture called pig swill.

Auction market

Live animals are taken to market by the farmer. Cattle are sold one by one. Pigs and sheep are weighed and sold in groups.

Abattoir

The animals are killed, then stored until they are sold.

Most meat is sold direct to butchers. Some is taken to meat markets.

Cooking meat

Meat has to be cooked before we eat it, to destroy any germs in it and make it tender and tasty.

Roasting is a way of cooking the large pieces (joints) in the ▶ oven.

▲ Stewing is the best way to cook meat which is not very tender. The meat is cooked in liquid inside, or on top of, the cooker.

◀ Grilling is a good way of cooking small, tender pieces of meat such as chops.

▲ Frying is cooking meat in fat in a shallow pan.

▲ Stir-frying is similar to normal frying. You toss thin strips of meat in a wok.

▲ Barbecuing is when meat is cooked on a barbecue outside.

▲ Braising means frying meat quickly, then adding liquid. The pot is then covered and put in the oven or left on top of the cooker.

Meat markets

These sell meat to butchers. One famous market is Smithfield in London. Butchers often buy a whole body. This is called a carcass.

Butcher

The butcher cuts the carcass up to sell it. Other things such as sausages and beefburgers are also made out of the meat.

Non meat-eaters

Some people, called vegetarians, don't eat meat or fish. They may think it is wrong to kill, or dislike the way some animals are kept. Some have religious reasons. For example, Hindus don't eat beef, and Jews won't eat pork.

Vegetarians eat lots of fruit and vegetables.

Sugar and chocolate

Sugar and chocolate both come from plants. Below you can find out what happens to the plants after they are picked.

Sugar

Sugar comes from sugar cane or sugar beet plants. Below you can see what is done to the plants to make brown sugar.

Sugar cane

Sugar from cane and sugar from beet look and taste the same.

The juice inside the thick stalks contains all the sugar.

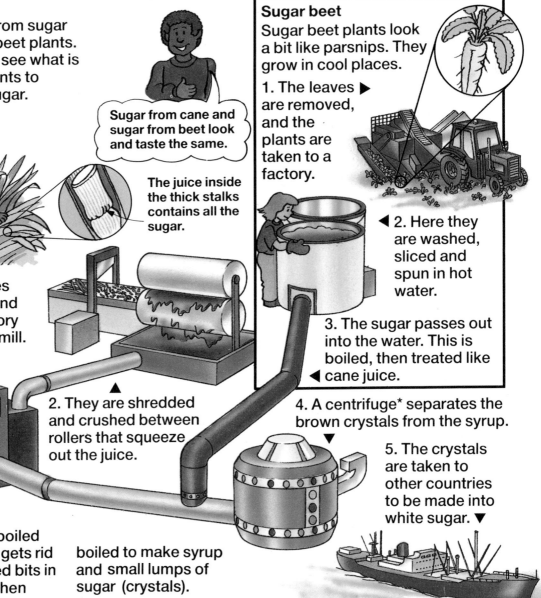

1. The tall canes are cut down and taken to a factory called a sugar mill.

2. They are shredded and crushed between rollers that squeeze out the juice.

Lime

3. The juice is boiled with lime. This gets rid of the unwanted bits in the juice. It is then boiled to make syrup and small lumps of sugar (crystals).

Sugar beet

Sugar beet plants look a bit like parsnips. They grow in cool places.

1. The leaves ▶ are removed, and the plants are taken to a factory.

◀ 2. Here they are washed, sliced and spun in hot water.

3. The sugar passes out into the water. This is boiled, then treated like ◀ cane juice.

4. A centrifuge* separates the brown crystals from the syrup.

5. The crystals are taken to other countries to be made into white sugar. ▼

You can find out about centrifuges on page 6.

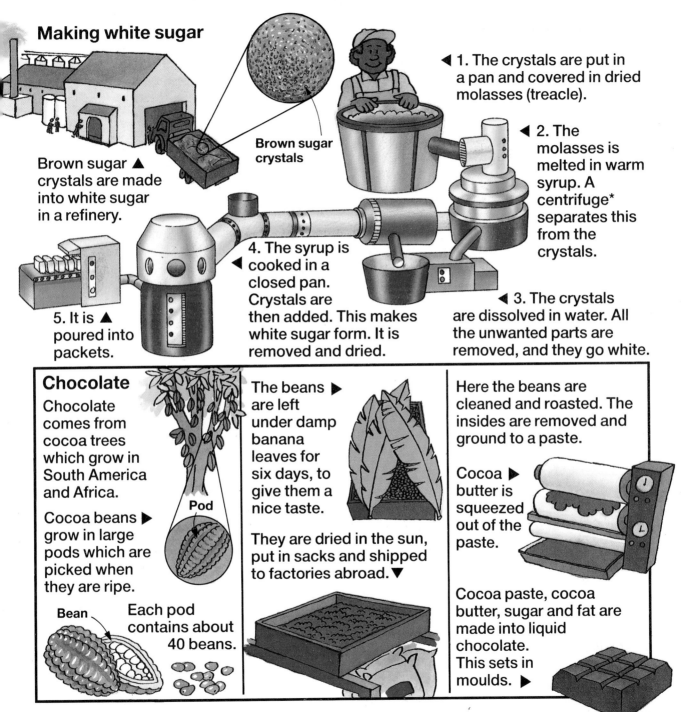

Making white sugar

Brown sugar crystals

Brown sugar ▲ crystals are made into white sugar in a refinery.

◀ 1. The crystals are put in a pan and covered in dried molasses (treacle).

◀ 2. The molasses is melted in warm syrup. A centrifuge* separates this from the crystals.

◀ 3. The crystals are dissolved in water. All the unwanted parts are removed, and they go white.

4. The syrup is ◀ cooked in a closed pan. Crystals are then added. This makes white sugar form. It is removed and dried.

5. It is ▲ poured into packets.

Chocolate

Chocolate comes from cocoa trees which grow in South America and Africa.

Cocoa beans ▶ grow in large pods which are picked when they are ripe.

Pod

Bean

Each pod contains about 40 beans.

The beans ▶ are left under damp banana leaves for six days, to give them a nice taste.

They are dried in the sun, put in sacks and shipped to factories abroad. ▼

Here the beans are cleaned and roasted. The insides are removed and ground to a paste.

Cocoa ▶ butter is squeezed out of the paste.

Cocoa paste, cocoa butter, sugar and fat are made into liquid chocolate. This sets in moulds. ▶

17

Breakfast cereal

Most breakfast cereals are made from crops which grow in fields. For example, muesli is made from oats. Below you can see how cornflakes are made.

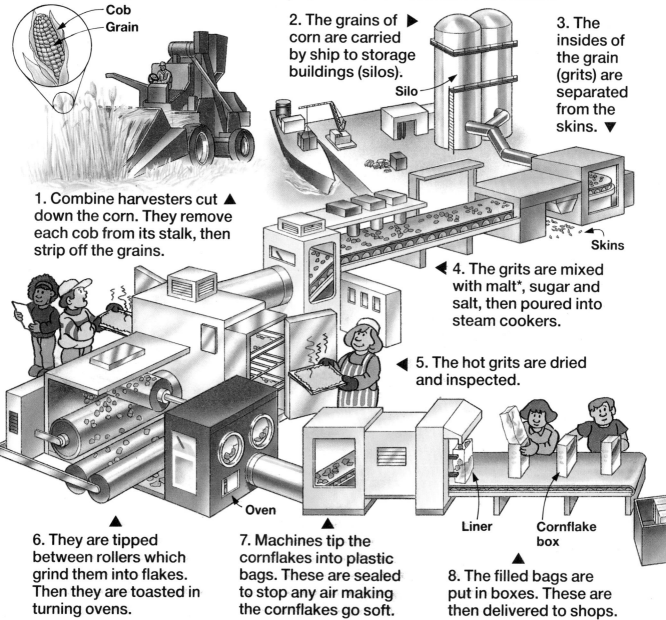

Cob
Grain

2. The grains of ▶ corn are carried by ship to storage buildings (silos).

Silo

3. The insides of the grain (grits) are separated from the skins. ▼

Skins

1. Combine harvesters cut ▲ down the corn. They remove each cob from its stalk, then strip off the grains.

4. The grits are mixed ◀ with malt*, sugar and salt, then poured into steam cookers.

5. The hot grits are dried ◀ and inspected.

Oven

Liner

Cornflake box

6. They are tipped between rollers which grind them into flakes. Then they are toasted in turning ovens.

7. Machines tip the cornflakes into plastic bags. These are sealed to stop any air making the cornflakes go soft.

8. The filled bags are put in boxes. These are then delivered to shops.

18   *Malt is barley that has sprouted and then been dried.

Pasta

Pasta is made out of semolina. This is wheat (see page 4) which has been rolled and sieved into even grains.

Below you can see how spaghetti is made.

Semolina

Mixer

Water

◀ 1. Semolina and water are tipped into a machine called an extruder.

2. The extruder pushes it through tiny holes which split it into long strands of wet spaghetti. ▼

Extruder

To extrude means to push out.

◀ 3. The spaghetti is now hung on rods and left to dry.

4. When the spaghetti is dry and hard, it is cut and put in packets. ▼

Other sorts of pasta

The extruder can make pasta in all sorts of shapes and sizes. A few are shown here.

Lasagne

Rigatoni

Spaghetti

Rings

Waggon wheels

Stars

Macaroni

Macaroni

For macaroni, the extruder has larger holes than those for spaghetti. There is a pin in the middle of each hole. This makes holes in the macaroni.

Tinned spaghetti

Some spaghetti is sent to factories. Here it is cooked, chopped up and put into cans with tomato sauce.

19

Rice

90% of the world's rice is grown and eaten in China and the East. The rest comes from the USA. In the USA, modern machines are used. These make rice-growing quick and efficient. In China and the East, rice is still grown by hand, as shown below.

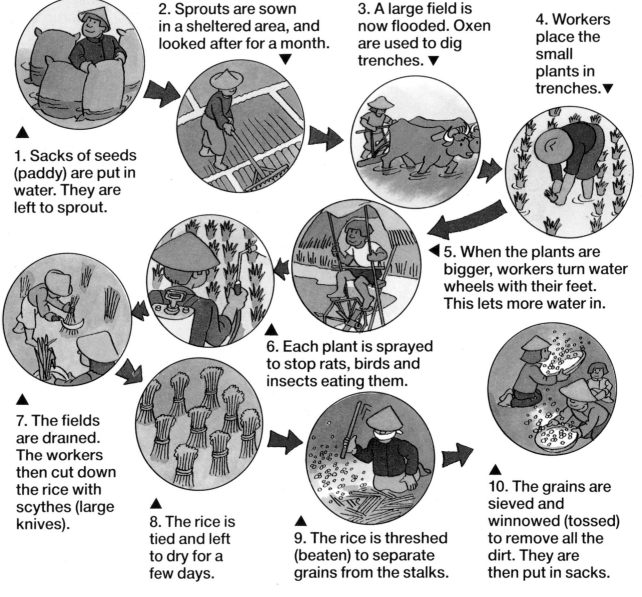

1. Sacks of seeds (paddy) are put in water. They are left to sprout.

2. Sprouts are sown in a sheltered area, and looked after for a month. ▼

3. A large field is now flooded. Oxen are used to dig trenches. ▼

4. Workers place the small plants in trenches. ▼

5. When the plants are bigger, workers turn water wheels with their feet. This lets more water in.

6. Each plant is sprayed to stop rats, birds and insects eating them.

7. The fields are drained. The workers then cut down the rice with scythes (large knives).

8. The rice is tied and left to dry for a few days.

9. The rice is threshed (beaten) to separate grains from the stalks.

10. The grains are sieved and winnowed (tossed) to remove all the dirt. They are then put in sacks.

The first American rice

In 1694, a ship carrying rice and spices was sailing from Madagascar. A storm blew up, and the ship had to shelter in Charleston, USA.

The captain gave the people some sacks of rice seed. They planted this seed, and soon there was enough rice for everyone in South Carolina.

Different sorts of rice

There are three main sorts of rice:
★ Long grain rice is good with savoury dishes such as curry.
★ Medium grain rice is used for both savoury and sweet dishes.
★ Short grain rice is good for rice puddings.

Make your own rice pudding

This recipe makes a thick, creamy pudding with a sugary skin on top. You will need:

100 g short grain rice

850 ml milk

75 g sugar

2 eggs (optional)

1. Heat the oven to Gas Mark 2.*

2. Heat the rice and milk in a saucepan.

3. Let the rice simmer for 10 minutes.

4. Let the rice cool. Beat the eggs in a bowl.

5. Mix everything together and put in a dish.

6. Bake in the oven for about half an hour.

*Electric ovens: 150°C or 300°F.

21

Drinks

Below you can find out how fizzy drinks are made.

You can also see where coffee and tea come from.

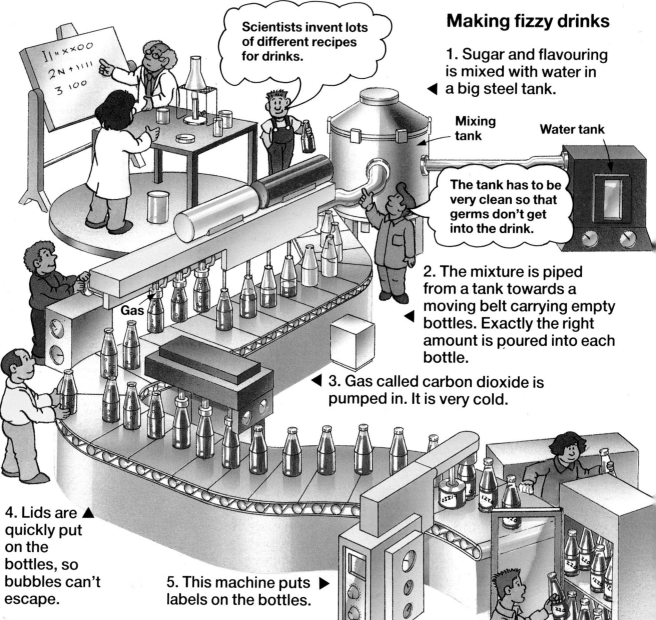

Scientists invent lots of different recipes for drinks.

Making fizzy drinks

1. Sugar and flavouring is mixed with water in a big steel tank.

Mixing tank

Water tank

The tank has to be very clean so that germs don't get into the drink.

Gas

2. The mixture is piped from a tank towards a moving belt carrying empty bottles. Exactly the right amount is poured into each bottle.

3. Gas called carbon dioxide is pumped in. It is very cold.

4. Lids are quickly put on the bottles, so bubbles can't escape.

5. This machine puts labels on the bottles.

The life of a coffee bean

Unripe berry
Ripe cherry
Branch of cherries
Coffee seeds

Over 4000 cherries are needed for 200g of coffee.

▲
1. Berries from coffee trees are dark green at first. As they ripen they go yellow, then they turn deep red and are called cherries.

▲
2. The cherries are picked or left until they fall off the trees. They are then collected and sifted to remove the dust, leaves and twigs.

Pulper

60kg sacks

▲
3. A machine removes the flesh (pulp). The outsides are washed, dried and put in a machine called a huller. The parts that are left are called beans.

▲
4. Sacks of beans are shipped abroad.
The beans are roasted. Some are sold whole. Others are ground into granules or powder.

Where does coffee grow?

Coffee trees need plenty of warm weather. If it is too hot or cold, they will die.

TROPIC OF CANCER
North America, Europe, Africa, South America, Australia
TROPIC OF CAPRICORN

Most coffee is grown between the Tropic of Cancer and the Tropic of Capricorn.

Tea

Tea leaves grow on bushes mainly in China and India.
Before modern ships were built, tea was carried to many countries in ships called clippers.

Tea clipper

23

Food facts

Milk, cheese and butter

★The top five butter producers are:

	(Tonnes per year)
USSR	1,290,000
India	730,000
France	600,000
USA	595,000
W. Germany	530,000

★87.7% of milk is water.

★The largest cheese ever made weighed 15,190kg. A tractor trailer 3.71m long was made especially to carry it.

Fruit and vegetables

★The largest crisp ever was 10cm x 17cm. It was made from a giant potato.

★The longest banana split was 7,060m. It was made from over 35,000 bananas.

★The hottest spice is the chilli pepper.

★The record for eating baked beans with a cocktail stick is 2,780 in 30 minutes.

★The oldest method of preservation is drying. Dried fruit was found in the tombs of the ancient kings of Egypt.

Fish

★The largest Paella (a Spanish fish and rice meal) was 10m wide and 45cm deep. It fed 15,000 people.

★About 81 million tonnes of fish are caught every year. Japan catches most – about 12 million tonnes.

Rice

★Over half the people living in the world eat more rice than anything else.

Meat

★A sausage maker in Birmingham, Britain made a sausage 9km long – that's about 87,000 ordinary sausages.

★Mr Boyer made the first meat substitute (something used instead of meat that looks and tastes very much like it) from soya beans about 50 years ago.

Breakfast cereals

★The first cornflakes were made by Mr Kellogg at Michigan, USA in 1902.

★Mr Graham (USA) invented the first breakfast cereal. He called it Graham Crackers.

Sugar and chocolate

★More than 100 million tonnes of sugar is eaten every year.

★The largest chocolate model ever made was of the design for the Olympic centre for the 1992 Olympics in Barcelona, Spain. It measured 10m x 5m and was 73cm high.

Drinks

★The average adult in Britain drinks about 1,650 cups of tea every year – about 4-5 cups a day.

★People in Finland drink the most coffee (12.9kg each per year). The Japanese drink least (1.62kg each).

HOW THINGS ARE MADE

Felicity Brooks

Edited by Janet Cook

Designed by Chris Scollen

**Illustrated by
Guy Smith and Teri Gower**

Contents

What are things made from?

Many natural things in the world around us are very useful. We can use parts of plants and animals, earth, rocks, trees, oil, gas and so on to make into the things we need. Today most things are made in factories. Lots can be made in a short time.

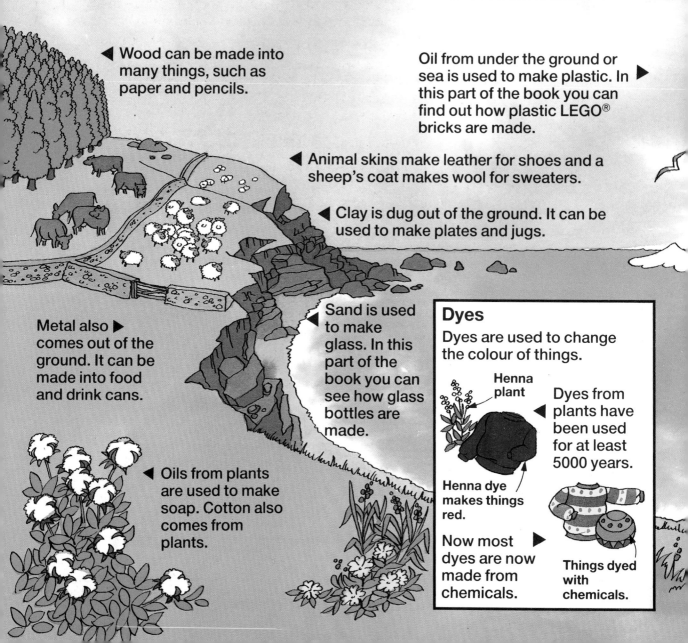

◀ Wood can be made into many things, such as paper and pencils.

Oil from under the ground or sea is used to make plastic. In this part of the book you can find out how plastic LEGO® bricks are made. ▶

◀ Animal skins make leather for shoes and a sheep's coat makes wool for sweaters.

◀ Clay is dug out of the ground. It can be used to make plates and jugs.

Metal also ▶ comes out of the ground. It can be made into food and drink cans.

◀ Sand is used to make glass. In this part of the book you can see how glass bottles are made.

◀ Oils from plants are used to make soap. Cotton also comes from plants.

Dyes

Dyes are used to change the colour of things.

Henna plant

◀ Dyes from plants have been used for at least 5000 years.

Henna dye makes things red.

Now most dyes are now made from chemicals. ▶

Things dyed with chemicals.

People drill for oil from oil rigs far out at sea.

Chemicals

Everything around us is made of chemicals – land, sea, air, houses, rocks, oil and even our bodies.

Scientists can separate ▶ out the chemicals in things like oil, rocks and plants and use them to make the things we need.

Medicines, plastic, paint and glue are made from chemicals.

Smoke coming out of a chemical factory.

◀ These chemicals are made in factories. They are very useful, but the smoke from the factories can be harmful.

Running out of power

Power is needed to run machines, cars and lorries. Power comes from things like gas, oil, coal and petrol.

What would happen if we ran out of petrol?

▲ Some scientists believe that we will run out of oil in about 100 years' time.

If we could find ways of using all the power from the waves, wind, water and sun, we would have 20 billion times more power than we need.▼

Wind turbines can make power from the wind.

Recycling

Cans, bottles and paper needn't be thrown away. They can be collected, taken to a factory and used to make new things.

Putting bottles in a bottle bank.

This is called recycling. It means we use less power, wood, chemicals and so on.

Leather shoes

Shoes can be made out of many different materials, such as leather, plastic or canvas. Leather is good because it stops feet getting too hot.

Leather is made from animal skin. The skin of a large animal like a cow is called a hide. It has to be treated in a factory to stop it from rotting.

Making leather

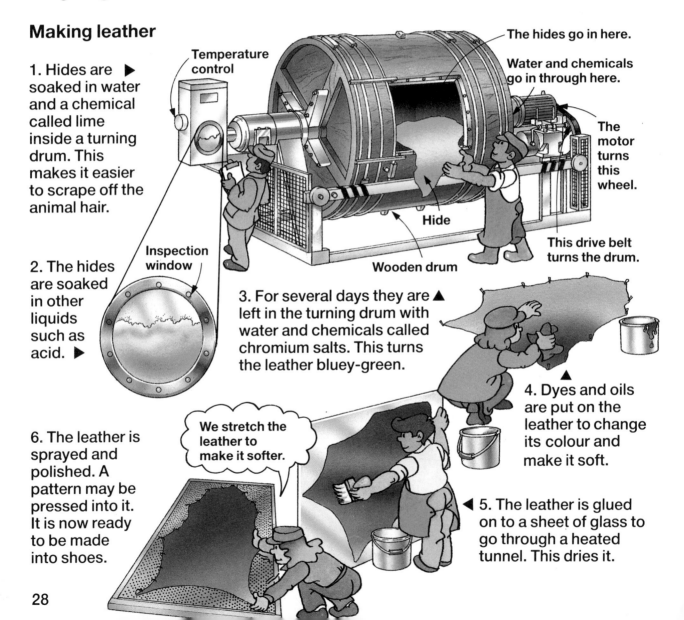

1. Hides are ▶ soaked in water and a chemical called lime inside a turning drum. This makes it easier to scrape off the animal hair.

Temperature control

The hides go in here.

Water and chemicals go in through here.

The motor turns this wheel.

Hide

This drive belt turns the drum.

Wooden drum

2. The hides are soaked in other liquids such as acid. ▶

Inspection window

3. For several days they are ▲ left in the turning drum with water and chemicals called chromium salts. This turns the leather bluey-green.

4. Dyes and oils are put on the leather to change its colour and make it soft.

6. The leather is sprayed and polished. A pattern may be pressed into it. It is now ready to be made into shoes.

We stretch the leather to make it softer.

◀ 5. The leather is glued on to a sheet of glass to go through a heated tunnel. This dries it.

28

Making a shoe

Shoes are made on models of feet called lasts. This picture shows the parts of the shoe.

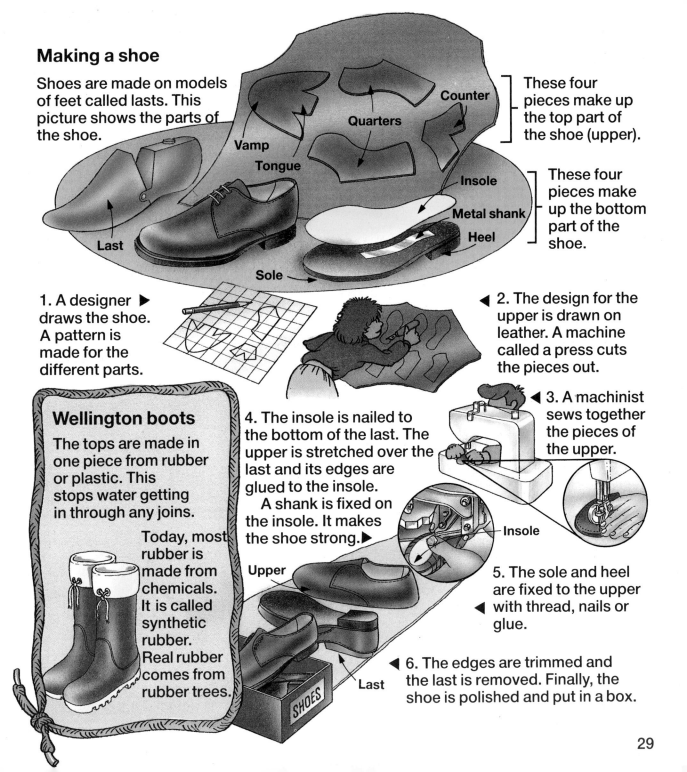

Vamp

Tongue

Quarters

Counter

These four pieces make up the top part of the shoe (upper).

Insole

Metal shank

Heel

These four pieces make up the bottom part of the shoe.

Last

Sole

1. A designer ▶ draws the shoe. A pattern is made for the different parts.

2. The design for the upper is drawn on leather. A machine called a press cuts the pieces out. ◀

3. A machinist sews together the pieces of the upper. ◀

4. The insole is nailed to the bottom of the last. The upper is stretched over the last and its edges are glued to the insole.

A shank is fixed on the insole. It makes the shoe strong. ▶

Insole

5. The sole and heel are fixed to the upper with thread, nails or glue. ◀

6. The edges are trimmed and the last is removed. Finally, the shoe is polished and put in a box. ◀

Upper

Last

SHOES

Wellington boots

The tops are made in one piece from rubber or plastic. This stops water getting in through any joins.

Today, most rubber is made from chemicals. It is called synthetic rubber. Real rubber comes from rubber trees.

29

Clay pottery

Clay can be shaped in many different ways. To make clay hard and waterproof, it must be baked in a very hot oven called a kiln and covered in a type of glass called glaze. This is how clay jugs are made in a factory.

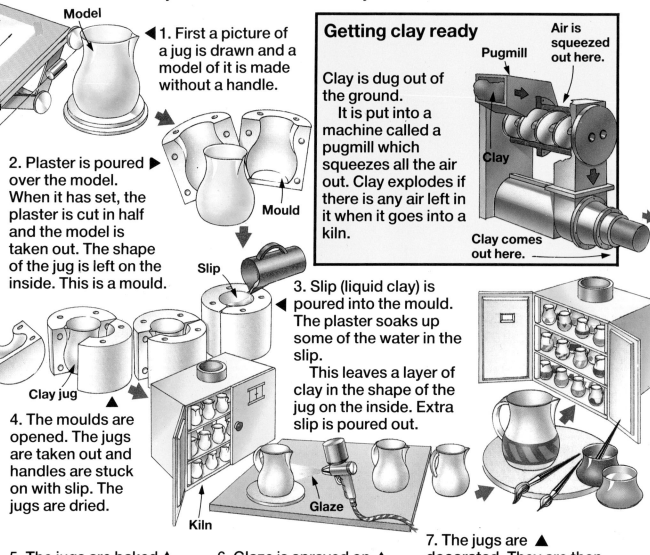

◀ 1. First a picture of a jug is drawn and a model of it is made without a handle.

Model

2. Plaster is poured ▶ over the model. When it has set, the plaster is cut in half and the model is taken out. The shape of the jug is left on the inside. This is a mould.

Mould

Getting clay ready

Clay is dug out of the ground.

It is put into a machine called a pugmill which squeezes all the air out. Clay explodes if there is any air left in it when it goes into a kiln.

Pugmill

Air is squeezed out here.

Clay

Clay comes out here.

Slip

3. Slip (liquid clay) is ◀ poured into the mould. The plaster soaks up some of the water in the slip.

This leaves a layer of clay in the shape of the jug on the inside. Extra slip is poured out.

Clay jug

4. The moulds are opened. The jugs are taken out and handles are stuck on with slip. The jugs are dried.

Kiln

Glaze

5. The jugs are baked ▲ (fired) in a kiln. This makes them hard.

6. Glaze is sprayed on ▲ the jugs. They are fired again.

7. The jugs are ▲ decorated. They are then fired again to stop the decorations washing off.

Making things by hand

The potter's wheel

The person who makes pots is called a potter. She can make them on a turning wheel, using her hands to make different shapes. This is called throwing.

▲ Getting a ball into the centre.

▲ Bringing up the sides of the pot.

▲ Shaping the neck of the pot.

Slab pots

Square pots can be made by cutting out pieces of clay and joining them together with slip. Pots made in this way are called slab pots.

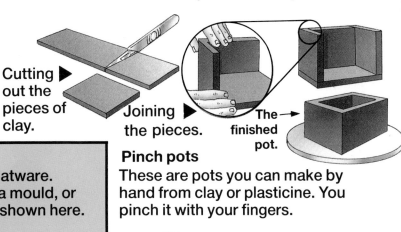

Cutting ▶ out the pieces of clay.

Joining ▶ the pieces.

The finished pot.

Plates

Plates and flat dishes are called flatware. They can be made on a wheel, in a mould, or by 'jiggering' with a metal tool as shown here.

A pancake of clay is put on a turning mould which shapes the plate.

▼

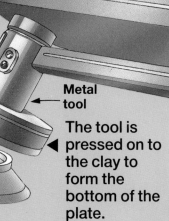

Clay

Plaster mould

Clay plate

Metal tool

The tool is pressed on to the clay to form the bottom of the plate.

Pinch pots

These are pots you can make by hand from clay or plasticine. You pinch it with your fingers.

◀ 1. Roll a ball in your hands. Make a hole in the middle with your thumb.

2. Turn the pot and ▶ squeeze the sides with your thumb and fingers.

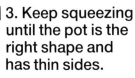

◀ 3. Keep squeezing until the pot is the right shape and has thin sides.

Woollen sweaters

Sweaters can be made from wool or synthetic fibres (see page 43), or a mixture of both. Woollen sweaters are the warmest.

Many things have to be done to the sheep's wool before it can be made into clothes.

Botany wool

Different sorts of wool come from different types of sheep. The finest sort is called Botany wool. It comes from Merino sheep.

Most Merino sheep live in Australia, Spain, South Africa and America.

Look in the label of your sweater to find out what it is made from.

There are a thousand million sheep in the world – that's one for every five people.

1. Shearing

The shearer cuts off the sheep's woollen coat with shears. He does this every year. It doesn't hurt the sheep.

2. Cleaning the wool

All sheep's wool is dirty. It has to be washed in the factory. ▶

3. Carding

The clean wool is untangled by a machine. This is called carding. The wool comes out in long strands ▶ called slivers.

4. Spinning

The spinning machine stretches the wool and twists the pieces together. This makes thread (yarn), ▶ which is wound on to bobbins.

Slivers

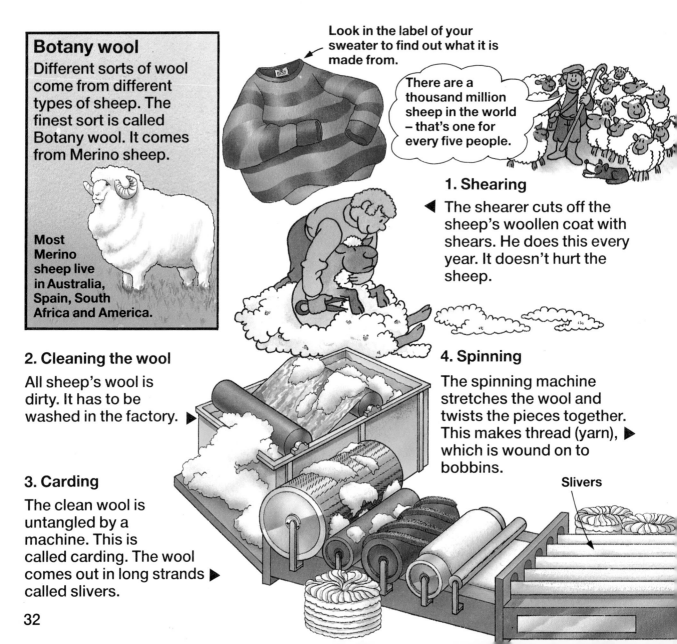

Woollen cloth

Other things like blankets and coats are also made from wool. Instead of being knitted, the yarn is woven into cloth on a machine called a loom.

Warp

Loom

Shuttle

Weft

A loom has one thread fixed lengthways up and down it. This is called the warp. Another thread (the weft) is fixed to a shuttle that moves backwards and forwards, under and over the warp.

Close-up of woven cloth.

Clothes from other animals

A camel's hair falls ▶ off in the spring. It is made into cloth for coats.

In South America, ▶ wool from llamas is used to make clothes and ropes.

Angora rabbits ▶ have fine silky fur that can be used to make soft, furry clothes.

Knitting machine

5. Dyeing

The bobbins are put into dye to change the colour of the yarn. When it is dry, the yarn can be made ▶ into a sweater.

Dye pan

Bobbin of yarn

Dye

Dyed yarn

Close-up of knitting

6. Knitting the sweater ▶

The pieces of the sweater are knitted on machines which can knit complicated patterns. They are sewn together on a sewing machine. The sweater is then pressed and packed.

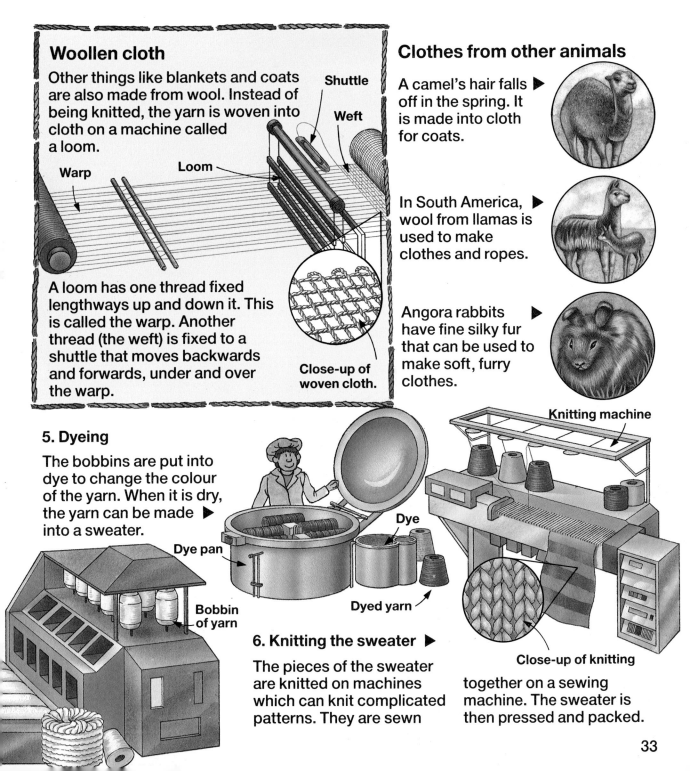

Reels of cotton

Cotton plants grow in hot countries such as India, China, Egypt and America.

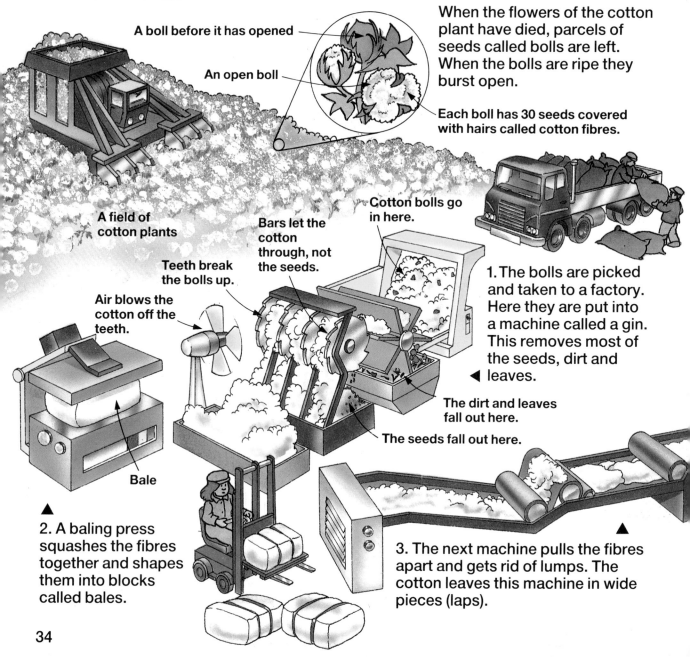

A boll before it has opened

An open boll

When the flowers of the cotton plant have died, parcels of seeds called bolls are left. When the bolls are ripe they burst open.

Each boll has 30 seeds covered with hairs called cotton fibres.

A field of cotton plants

Bars let the cotton through, not the seeds.

Teeth break the bolls up.

Air blows the cotton off the teeth.

Cotton bolls go in here.

1. The bolls are picked and taken to a factory. Here they are put into a machine called a gin. This removes most of the seeds, dirt and ◀ leaves.

The dirt and leaves fall out here.

The seeds fall out here.

Bale

▲
2. A baling press squashes the fibres together and shapes them into blocks called bales.

3. The next machine pulls the fibres apart and gets rid of lumps. The cotton leaves this machine in wide pieces (laps).

Making silk

Silk is a fine material. It comes from a caterpillar called a silkworm.

Silk scarf

Silkworms — Cocoon

It spins the threads around its body, making a thin shell (cocoon).

Before it turns into a moth, a silkworm squirts streams of liquid from tiny holes in its head. These dry and become fine threads of silk.

Each cocoon is unwound to make a fine thread. Several of these are twisted together and woven into material.

4. The laps are untangled (carded) and combed into long ropes called slivers. Several of these go into a machine that joins them and pulls them out into smaller laps. ▼

Speed frame

6. A spinning machine spins the cotton into fine yarn. Several threads of yarn are twisted together to make strong sewing thread. ▼

Spinning machine

Lap

Slivers

Lap

5. A machine called a speed frame pulls and twists the laps until each one is thinner than a pencil.

7. The thread is put into a chemical which makes it shiny. It is then bleached (for white thread), or dyed. Finally it is wound on to plastic reels.*

Cotton thread can also be woven (see page 33).

35

Paper

Most paper is made from wood. This comes from evergreen trees in North America and Scandinavia. Quick-growing gum trees in South America, Spain and Portugal are also used.

A forest the size of Wales is enough to supply the world with paper each year.

1. The trees are chopped ▶ down and the bark is taken off. A machine cuts the logs into 'chips' about 2cm long.

Chip

2. The chips are ▶ cooked in water and chemicals to break them up. The wood is now pulp.

3. To get rid of dirt ◀ and lumps, the pulp is washed. Next it is put into bleach to whiten it. Then it is washed again.

Dye added here. Beater

4. The pulp is beaten to ◀ break up the wood into tiny thin strands called fibres.

Paper machine

Pulp on moving belt.

5. The thick pulp is mixed with water. To ◀ make coloured paper, dye can be added.

6. The paper machine spreads ▲ out the pulp on a moving belt with millions of tiny holes in it. The belt jiggles from side to side, helping the fibres to stick together.

Suction boxes suck the water away. As it begins to dry out, the pulp becomes paper.

Rollers

Paper   Felt

7. It moves on to a layer of felt. Rollers squeeze more water out and press the fibres together.

8. Hot rollers dry the paper. It is wound on to rolls, then cut into pieces. ▶

Looking at paper fibres

Wood is made up of tiny strands called fibres. Cooking and adding chemicals to the wood and beating the pulp breaks the fibres up into tiny frayed pieces. When water is added and then removed, these stick together to make paper.

Beater

Pulp before beating

After some beating

After a lot of beating

Tear some paper. Can you see tiny whiskers on the edge? These are fibres.

Recycling paper

Waste paper can be dissolved in hot water to turn it back into pulp and used to make new paper or cardboard. This is called recycling. It uses less power and chemicals and fewer trees.

In Britain, half the pulp for new paper is made from used paper and cardboard.

Paper with wax or plastic on it cannot be recycled.

Boxes, magazines and newspapers can be recycled.

Making banknotes

The paper used for banknotes is made out of cotton because this is strong. The notes have to be difficult to copy, so they have a watermark and often a security thread in them.

Security thread

Watermark

You can see the watermark if you hold a note up to the light.

The watermark

The watermark is made by making the paper thicker in some places and thinner in others when it is still wet. Look out for them in other types of paper too.

An artist designs a new note. An engraver cuts the design into a sheet of steel. This is used to make printing plates with many copies of the design on each one.

Metal printing plate

Printing

A machine presses the inked plates on to paper to make a sheet of notes. It can make 9000 sheets an hour in up to eight colours.

The sheets are then cut into single notes and packed.

Sheet of notes

Printing machine

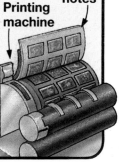

Glass bottles

Bottles, jars and many other everyday things are made out of glass. When glass is very hot it becomes soft and can be made into different shapes.

2000 years ago people found out how to blow air into hot glass to make hollow things. Now this can be done by machines.

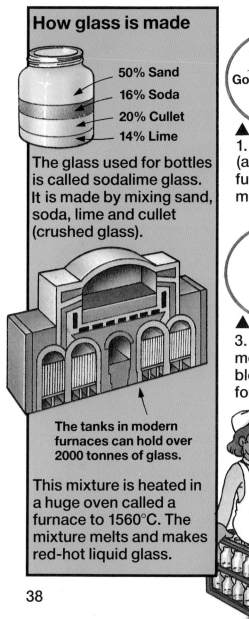

How glass is made

50% Sand
16% Soda
20% Cullet
14% Lime

The glass used for bottles is called sodalime glass. It is made by mixing sand, soda, lime and cullet (crushed glass).

The tanks in modern furnaces can hold over 2000 tonnes of glass.

This mixture is heated in a huge oven called a furnace to 1560°C. The mixture melts and makes red-hot liquid glass.

Gob

1. A lump of hot, soft glass (a gob) is taken from the furnace and dropped into a metal mould.

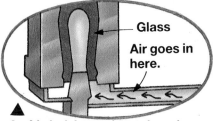

Glass

Air goes in here.

2. Air is blown into the glass. The bottle is then taken out of the mould and turned over.

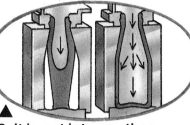

3. It is put into another mould and more air is blown in through the top to form the final shape.

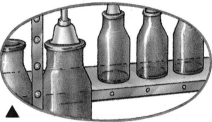

4. The glass bottle is taken out of the mould and put on a moving conveyor belt.

This machine can make over 200 bottles a minute.

The first automatic bottle-making machine was used in 1907.

Blowing glass

Until 100 years ago, blowing glass by mouth was the most usual way to shape things. Some people still do this.

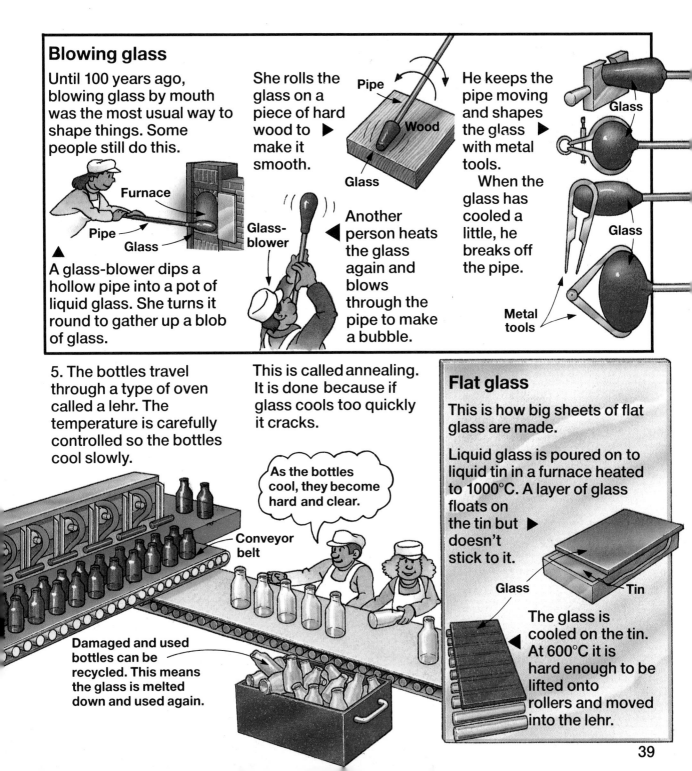

A glass-blower dips a hollow pipe into a pot of liquid glass. She turns it round to gather up a blob of glass.

Furnace
Pipe
Glass

She rolls the glass on a piece of hard wood to ▶ make it smooth.

Pipe
Wood
Glass

Glass-blower

Another person heats the glass again and blows through the pipe to make a bubble.

He keeps the pipe moving and shapes the glass ▶ with metal tools.

Glass

When the glass has cooled a little, he breaks off the pipe.

Glass

Metal tools

---

5. The bottles travel through a type of oven called a lehr. The temperature is carefully controlled so the bottles cool slowly.

This is called annealing. It is done because if glass cools too quickly it cracks.

As the bottles cool, they become hard and clear.

Conveyor belt

Damaged and used bottles can be recycled. This means the glass is melted down and used again.

Flat glass

This is how big sheets of flat glass are made.

Liquid glass is poured on to liquid tin in a furnace heated to 1000°C. A layer of glass floats on the tin but ▶ doesn't stick to it.

Glass
Tin

The glass is cooled on the tin. At 600°C it is hard enough to be lifted onto rollers and moved into the lehr.

Food and drink cans

Most food cans are made from tinplate which is flat steel covered with a very thin layer of the metal tin.

Tin doesn't rust, but it is too expensive to be used by itself. A thin layer stops steel rusting and spoiling the food.

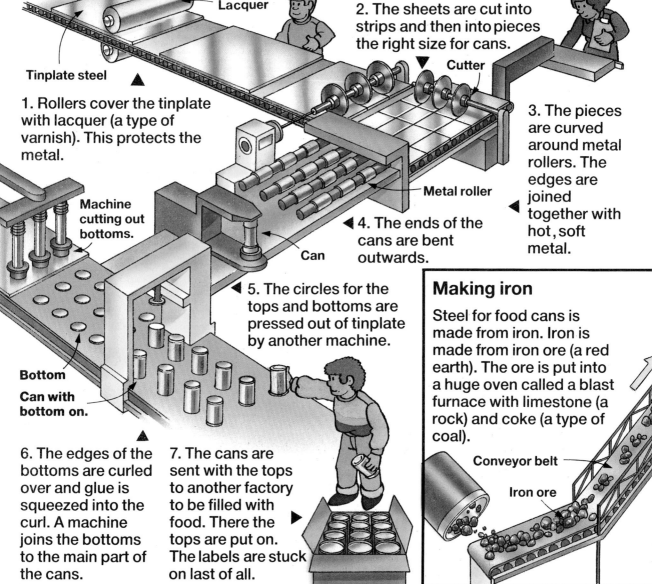

Lacquer

Tinplate steel ▲

1. Rollers cover the tinplate with lacquer (a type of varnish). This protects the metal.

2. The sheets are cut into strips and then into pieces the right size for cans.

Cutter ▼

3. The pieces are curved around metal rollers. The edges are joined together with hot, soft metal. ◄

Metal roller

Machine cutting out bottoms.

Can

◄ **4.** The ends of the cans are bent outwards.

◄ **5.** The circles for the tops and bottoms are pressed out of tinplate by another machine.

Bottom

Can with bottom on. ▲

6. The edges of the bottoms are curled over and glue is squeezed into the curl. A machine joins the bottoms to the main part of the cans.

7. The cans are sent with the tops to another factory to be filled with food. There the tops are put on. The labels are stuck on last of all. ►

Making iron

Steel for food cans is made from iron. Iron is made from iron ore (a red earth). The ore is put into a huge oven called a blast furnace with limestone (a rock) and coke (a type of coal).

Conveyor belt

Iron ore

Drink cans

Most drink cans are made from the metal aluminium which doesn't rust and is light and strong.

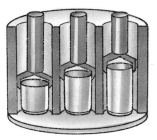

The bottom and sides are made on machines that can stretch one piece of metal upwards to make a can without a join.

The design is printed on after the can has been shaped.

The top is put on when the can has been filled.

Top

Can facts

In the USA, one million tonnes of aluminium are made into cans every year – the same weight as two of the world's largest ships.

This house in Lesotho, in Southern Africa is made from old cans and paint pots.

Now cans are thinner, you can make 7000 more cans from one tonne of aluminium than 10 years ago.

Old can
New can

Blast furnace

Gas comes out here.

Lining of furnace

Iron ore

Liquid iron

Hot air goes in here.

Slag

Liquid iron

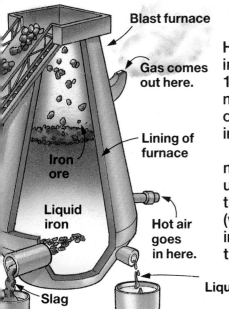

Hot air is blasted into the furnace. At 1500°C, the coke mixes with the iron ore to make liquid iron.

The limestone mixes with the unwanted things in the ore making slag (waste matter). The iron trickles out at the bottom .

Making steel

Most steel is made in a furnace by blowing oxygen into hot iron.

Oxygen goes in here.

Liquid steel

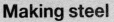

This makes liquid steel. The furnace can tip over and pour the steel out.

Steel for food cans can be rolled out flat while it is soft.

LEGO® bricks

Scientists separate out the different ingredients (chemicals) in things like oil, coal and gas and use them to make plastic. Different chemicals make different types of plastic.

Making plastic

Everything is made of millions of tiny parts called molecules. Each molecule is made up of even smaller parts called atoms. Plastic is made from some of the biggest molecules there are, but they are still too small to see.

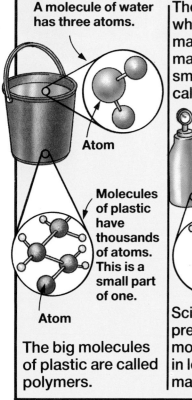

A molecule of water has three atoms.

Atom

Molecules of plastic have thousands of atoms. This is a small part of one.

Atom

The big molecules of plastic are called polymers.

The chemicals which are used to make plastic are made of much smaller molecules called monomers.

This is a monomer of a gas used to make plastic.

Scientists heat and press lots of these monomers together in long chains to make polymers.

Plastic is made in a factory called a chemical plant. When it leaves the plant, it looks like small coloured lumps. These are called granules. Some are made into LEGO bricks.

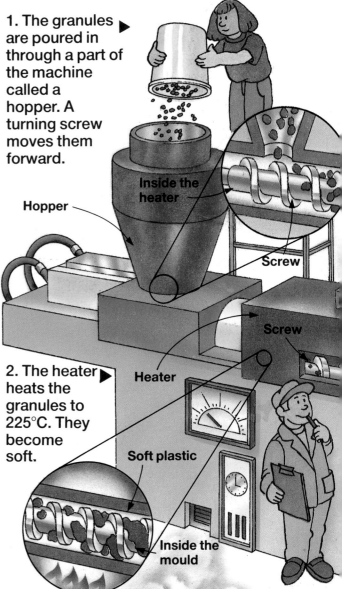

1. The granules ▶ are poured in through a part of the machine called a hopper. A turning screw moves them forward.

Inside the heater

Hopper

Screw

Screw

2. The heater ▶ heats the granules to 225°C. They become soft.

Heater

Soft plastic

Inside the mould

Plastic clothes

Some of the clothes you are wearing may be made from materials such as nylon or polyester or acrylic. These are called synthetic fibres. They are sorts of plastic.

Acrylic sweater

Nylon tights

Polyester shirts

Some materials, such as viscose, are plastics made from chemicals mixed with natural things like wood and cotton. These are called man-made fibres.

Viscose is made from wood pulp.

Viscose skirt

These fibres are made by pushing liquid plastic through holes in a machine called a spinneret.

Scientists got the idea for this by watching silkworms (see page 35).

Spinneret

Tiny holes

These thin plastic threads are hardened in warm or cool air, or in acid, depending on the material.

Spinneret

Cool air

Liquid plastic

Threads are twisted together to make strong thread for clothes.

Look at the labels on your clothes. How many man-made or synthetic fibres can you spot? Clues on page 74.

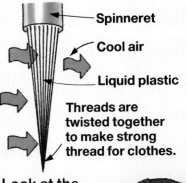

100% ACRYLIC

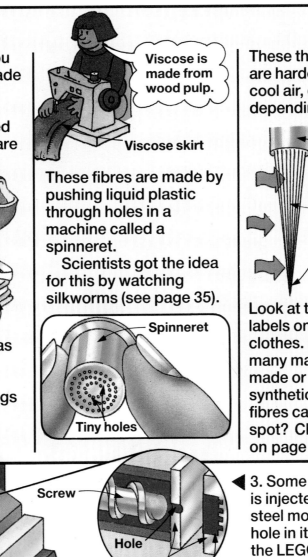

Screw

Hole

Mould

New LEGO brick

◀ 3. Some of the soft plastic is injected into a cold steel mould that has a hole in it in the shape of the LEGO brick.

◀ 4. The plastic cools and hardens in the shape of the mould. The mould is opened up and a LEGO brick falls out into a box.

The LEGO bricks come out here.

43

Bars of soap

Bars of soap are made from fats and oils mixed with a chemical called caustic soda. Until 30 years ago soap-making was done in open pans and took a week . Now it can be done in a few hours by machines that work non-stop.

A big soap factory makes a million bars a day.

Fats and oils in soap

Castor oil	5%
Palm oil	10%
Coconut oil	25%
Animal fat	60%

Oils from plants and fat from animals can be used to make soap.

1. The caustic soda, fat and oil are boiled together in a closed pan. The pan works like a pressure cooker. It cooks the soap in 15 minutes.

Boiling pan

Salty water

2. The soap has glycerine (a chemical) in it. This isn't needed, so salty water is added. Glycerine mixes with the water, but the soap doesn't.

Centrifuge

3. A machine called a centrifuge spins the mixture very fast. This separates the glycerine mixture from the soap.

Glycerine

Fitting column

How soap works

Soap is made up of millions of tiny parts called molecules. Each molecule has two parts – a head and a tail.

Head

Soap

Tail

Water

Dirt

Skin

The head likes water, the tail doesn't. The tails stick to the dirt on your skin when you wash, and pull it away.

4. A machine called a fitting column removes any other chemicals that aren't needed in the soap.

44

Soap long ago

Today soap is quite cheap and there are lots of colours and types to choose from. 400 years ago soap was very expensive, didn't smell nice and was only dirty brown or grey.

Some people used to make their own soap by boiling a mixture of fat and ash.

In those days, people didn't wash very often. Queen Elizabeth 1 of England (1588 – 1603) only had a bath once a month – more often than most people.

Elizabeth 1

Soap noodles coming out of the refiner.

7. Perfume and colour are added to the noodles.

8. The noodles are pressed together and dried some more to make large rectangular pieces.

Refiners

Perfume

Rectangular pieces of soap

6. The soap goes through two refining machines which clean it. The second machine divides the soap into little lumps called noodles.

Spray drier

Cold air

9. The soap is cut into bars. These go through a tunnel of cold air to make them firm.

Soap

5. The liquid soap has now cooled a little. A spray drier heats and dries it to make it more solid.

10. A stamper makes a pattern on the bars of soap. They are then wrapped and packed in boxes.

SOAP

45

Pencils, paint, tape and toothpaste

On these pages you can find out how a few more everyday things are made.

Wooden pencils

1. The leads are made from ground-up graphite (a sort of ▶ soft rock), clay and water. This soft mixture is pressed through a small hole to make thin sticks.

2. The sticks are cut, dried and baked in a hot oven (kiln).

Leads

Kiln

◀ 3. The wood is cut into flat strips. A machine makes three grooves in each strip. The leads are put in the grooves.

Grooves

Join

Lead

Paint

Stamp

4. Another strip of grooved wood is glued on top. The strips are pressed together firmly.

5. A machine cuts the wood into three pieces and shapes these into pencils. They are then painted.

6. A machine stamps on the maker's name and type of pencil. The pencils are sharpened and packed.

Types of pencil

More graphite in the lead makes a pencil softer. More clay makes it harder. You can see how hard a pencil is by looking at the code printed on its side. The most common is HB.

4B	Soft and black
B	Black
HB	Hard and black
H	Hard
2H	Hard
4H	Very hard
7H	Extra hard

Sticky tape

The tape is a type of plastic. The sticky stuff (adhesive) is made from synthetic rubber and resin.*

Liquid is put on one side of the tape. This will make it easier to unroll.

A machine puts a very thin layer of adhesive on the other side of the tape.

Liquid   **Oven**

*Real resin is sap (a liquid from inside trees). Synthetic resin is made from chemicals.

Paint

Paint is made from pigment (a powder) and binder (a liquid). The pigment gives the paint its colour.

◀ Pigments can be made from things such as rocks and plants or from chemicals.

The binder is often ▶ varnish made from vegetable oil mixed with real or synthetic resin*. It can also be a type of plastic.

Paint mixer

Paint

◀ All the ingredients are measured and mixed in a machine for many hours, before being put into tins, pots or tubes.

When you use paint, the binder dries to a solid layer that keeps the pigment in place.

Toothpaste

These ingredients are put in a sealed metal mixer for three hours.

1. Polisher: powder made from bauxite (a sort of rock).
2. Humectant: stops paste drying up. Made from maize.
3. Binder: keeps paste well mixed. Made from wood pulp.
4. Detergent: cleans teeth and makes paste foamy. Made from chemicals.
5. Germicide: chemical for killing germs in paste.
6. Fluoride: chemical that helps keep teeth strong.
7. Flavour: makes paste taste nice. Made from plants such as mint.
8. Saccharin: makes paste sweet. Chemical made from coal.

The lids of the tubes are put on. The bottoms are left open. A machine fills each tube with paste. The ends are sealed by another machine.

1
2
3
4
5
6
7
8

After each layer the tape goes through ovens to dry.

Jumbo roll

Oven

Tape

The adhesive cools and becomes solid and sticky. The tape is wound to make a 'jumbo roll.'

Finally, the tape is cut and wound on to smaller rolls.
    A large factory can make enough tape in a week to cover 1000 swimming pools.

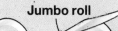

Facts and dates

Shoes

★Shoe sizes were first used in 1792, in England. Before that, each pair of shoes was made specially for a particular person.

★The most expensive shoes were bought by Emperor Bokassa of Africa for his coronation. They cost £38,000 (US $85,000).

Glass

★The first glass was made 5000 years ago in the Middle East.

★The largest bottle is a 1.83m whisky bottle that can hold 185 litres (41 gallons) – about the same as 555 cans of drink.

★Mr Pilkington invented the method for making flat sheets of glass (see page 39) in 1952.
The largest sheet of glass ever made was 20m x 2.5m.

Pottery

★The first potter's wheel (see page 31) was used about 5,500 years ago. It was a flat table spun round by hand.

Silk

★To make 1kg of silk, silkworms need to eat 220kg of Mulberry leaves.

★Silk is so fine that it takes 3000 cocoons to make 1m of silk material.

Cotton

★Pieces of cotton 8000 years old have been found in a cave in Mexico.

★People only began to use cotton for sewing about 150 years ago. Before that silk or linen thread was used.

★The top five cotton producers are:

	(Tonnes per year)
China	5,700,000
USA	2,913,000
USSR	2,400,000
India	1,250,000
Pakistan	860,000

Metal

★The largest steel company is in Japan. It makes 27 million tonnes of steel a year.

Wool

★The top five wool producers are:

	(Tonnes per year)
Australia	722,000
USSR	460,000
New Zealand	363,000
China	205,000
Argentina	155,000

★In Australia there are about nine times as many sheep as people. There are 15 million people. How many sheep is that ?*

Paper

★The Chinese made the first paper from wood, cotton and straw about 2000 years ago.

★412 newspapers can be made from one tree. About 14 million copies of the Japanese newspaper Yomiuri Shimbun are sold every day using paper from about 34,000 trees.

Plastic

★The first plastic was made in 1862. It was called Parkesine.

★The first man-made fibre (rayon) was made in 1884.

HOW THINGS ARE BUILT

Helen Edom

Edited by Janet Cook

Designed by Robert Walster and Chris Scollen

Illustrated by Guy Smith, Teri Gower and Chris Lyon

Consultant: Peter Wright BSc (Eng) Hons. C Eng M.I.C.E.

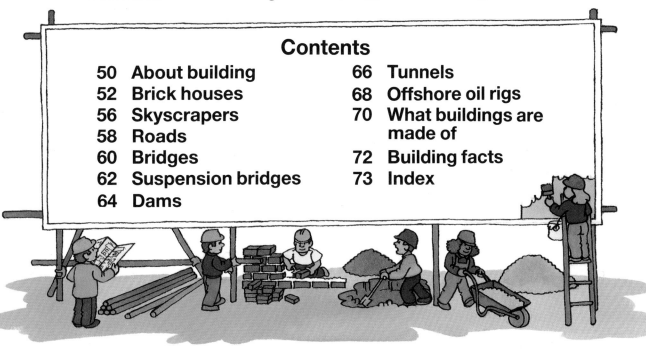

Contents

About building

This book shows you how buildings such as houses, roads and bridges are built.

On the right are some of the different sorts of builders you will meet in this book.

The person who makes walls out of bricks is called a bricklayer.

The person who makes things with wood is called a carpenter.

What are buildings made of?

Buildings are made out of strong things such as concrete, steel and wood. You can find out more about these on pages 70-71.

This diver dives into the sea to work on the underneath of an oil rig.

This person is called a welder. He uses a very hot tool to join metal pieces.

The story of building

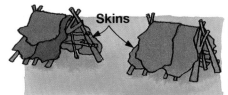

A million years ago, people built huts from branches. They hung animal skins over them to keep out rain.

Later, they moved blocks of stone by dragging them over tree trunks. They kept moving the trunks to the front of the stone.

About 4000 years ago, the Egyptians built stone pyramids. They made earth slopes so they could drag stone blocks up to the top.

How buildings begin

Once somebody has had an idea for a building, a plan is drawn to show how it is to be built.

Plan

Engineers draw plans for buildings like bridges. They make sure these buildings don't fall down.

NOTE
All the buildings in this book can be built in many different ways. Usually only one way of building is shown.

Architects draw plans for houses and offices. They work with engineers if the building is big.

Architects like to think of ways to make buildings attractive and pleasant to work in or live in.

When the plans are finished, a copy is given to the builders. The builders can then start.

Column

Over 2000 years ago, Greeks and Romans used stone columns to hold up buildings. The Romans are also famous for roads.

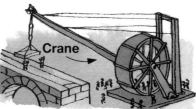

Crane

600 years ago, builders used cranes to lift loads. This helped them to build tall buildings like bridges and churches.

Now we have modern machines, twenty skyscrapers can be built in the same time that it took to build one pyramid.

Brick houses

Houses are built in many different ways. The builders you can see at work here and on the next two pages are building with bricks, concrete and wood. See if you can find out what your house is made from.

Preparing to build

The plan on the right shows what the house will look like and how big it is going to be.

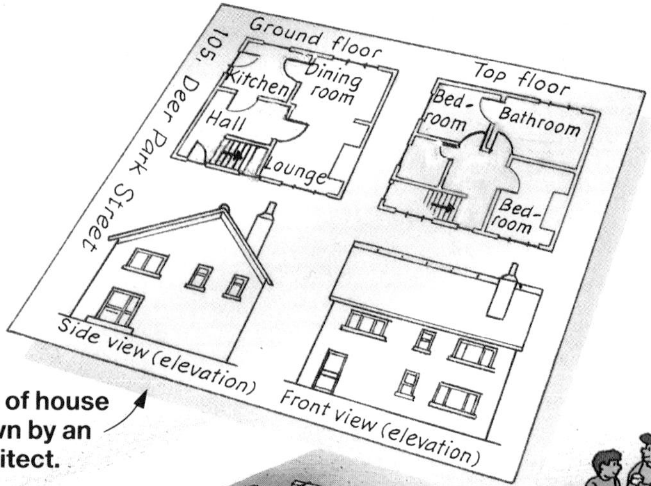

Plan of house drawn by an architect.

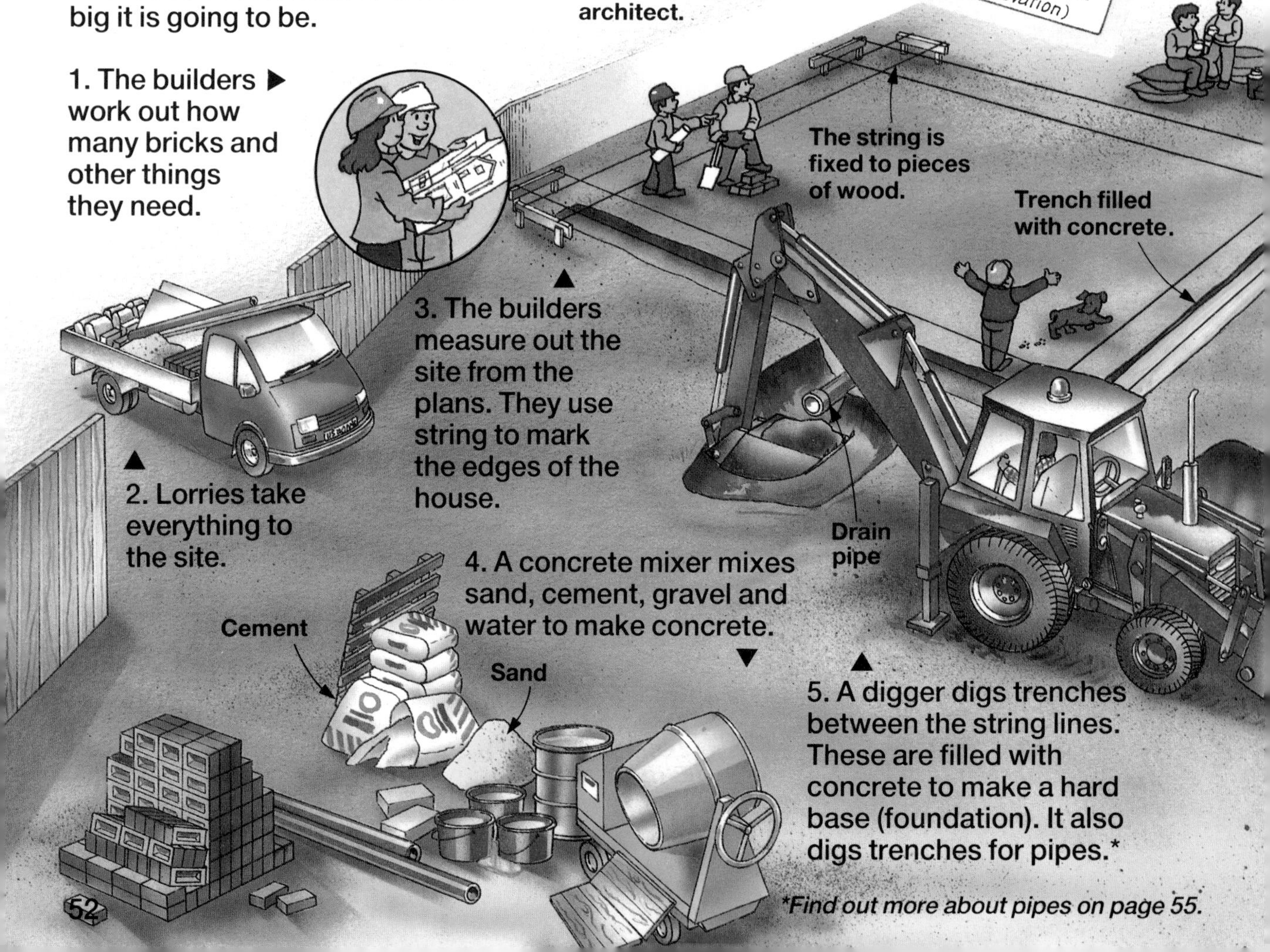

1. The builders ▶ work out how many bricks and other things they need.

The string is fixed to pieces of wood.

Trench filled with concrete.

3. The builders measure out the site from the plans. They use string to mark the edges of the house.

2. Lorries take everything to the site.

Drain pipe

4. A concrete mixer mixes sand, cement, gravel and water to make concrete. ▼

Cement

Sand

5. A digger digs trenches between the string lines. These are filled with concrete to make a hard base (foundation). It also digs trenches for pipes.*

*Find out more about pipes on page 55.

52

Building the walls

Bricklayers build walls on the foundation. First they make the corners and put string between them. This helps them build straight.

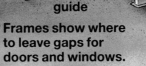

Concrete blocks

String guide

Frames show where to leave gaps for doors and windows.

Concrete block

A trowel is used to spread mortar between bricks.

The bricks are stuck together with mortar (see page 71).

The walls inside the house are made from big concrete blocks.

See for yourself

Try this experiment to see how important the damp-proof course is.

1. Dip some kitchen paper in water. The water goes up it.

Wet **Dry**

2. Cut another piece in half. Tape the halves together with a small gap between them.

Tape

Gap

3. Dip it in water. The water cannot go above the waterproof tape.

Wet **Dry**

Water goes up through floors and walls in this way, unless stopped by a waterproof layer.

Keeping water out of the house

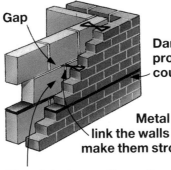

Gap

Damp-proof course

Metal ties link the walls and make them strong.

The air between the walls helps keep the house warm and dry.

◀ Another wall is built about 6cm inside the outer wall.

The bricklayer puts waterproof bitumenised felt (see page 70) in both walls, just above the ground. This stops water soaking up. It is called a damp-proof course.

Building the floor

The ground inside the ▶ walls is dug out. Concrete is poured over layers of stones, sand and plastic. The plastic stops water rising into the floor.

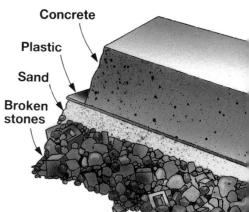

Concrete

Plastic

Sand

Broken stones

Building the upstairs

1. Builders lay pieces of wood (joists) from one wall to the other.

2. They nail wooden floorboards on top of the joists to make the floor.

3. They nail plasterboards (see page 71) underneath the joists. This makes a ceiling for the downstairs rooms.

Joists

Ceiling

Floorboards

Scaffolding

Scaffolding

Scaffolding is like a huge climbing frame made from steel tubes. Builders stand on planks laid across it to reach the top of the house.

Clamps are tightened around the tubes to fix them together.

Bolt

Plasterboard

Houses with frames

The brick house on this page is held up by its walls. Other houses are held up by wooden, concrete or metal frames.

This often happens in the USA.

A wooden house which is held up by its frame can be moved on a lorry.

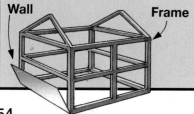

Wall

Frame

Upstairs rooms ▲

Plasterboards are used to divide the upstairs area into rooms.

Making the stairs ▶

The carpenter builds the staircase. The top of each step is called a tread. The upright pieces are called risers.

Putting the roof on

1. The frame for the roof is made from wooden triangular shapes. They rest on the walls.

2. Roofing felt is spread over the frame. Strips of wood are nailed on top.

3. Overlapping tiles are nailed to the strips. Rain runs off them and into the guttering.

The tiles used along the top are called ridge tiles.

Battens

Roofing felt

Guttering

Floorboards

Riser

Tread

Building the chimney

The chimney is built up through the roof. A metal strip (flashing) is bent round it. This stops rain leaking between the chimney and tiles.

Flashing

Finishing off

★ A glazier puts glass in the windows.

★ An electrician lays wiring.

★ A plasterer covers the walls with plaster.

★ A decorator paints the house.

Laying the water pipes

A plumber joins pipes together to carry water around the house.

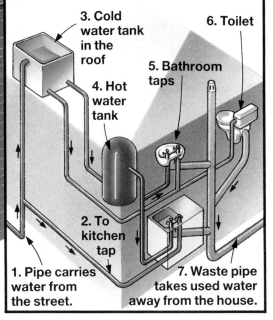

3. Cold water tank in the roof

6. Toilet

5. Bathroom taps

4. Hot water tank

2. To kitchen tap

1. Pipe carries water from the street.

7. Waste pipe takes used water away from the house.

55

Skyscrapers

A skyscraper is built on a huge frame. This is fixed to a strong base (foundation).

Skyscraper foundations

A skyscraper is very heavy, so it needs a strong foundation. It has legs, called piles, which go deep into the earth.

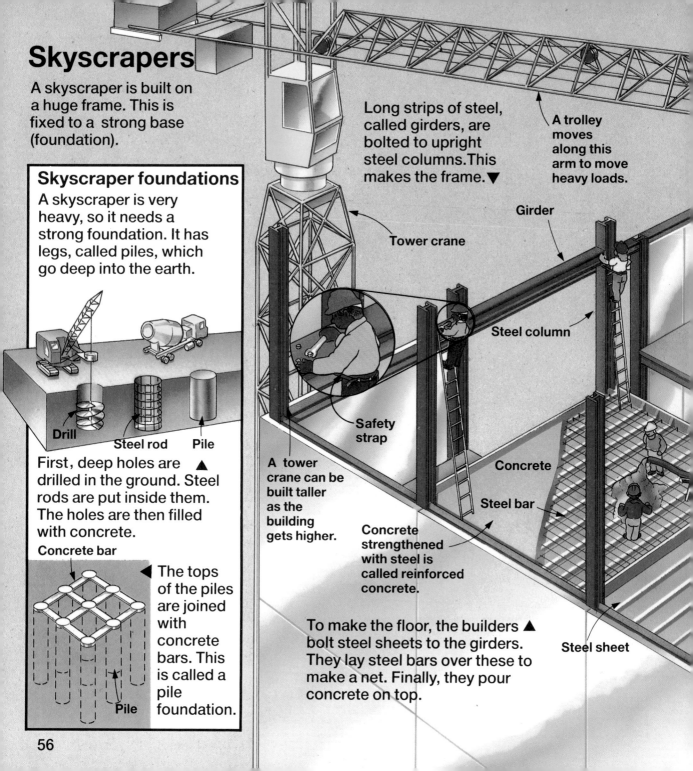

Drill   **Steel rod**   **Pile**

First, deep holes are ▲ drilled in the ground. Steel rods are put inside them. The holes are then filled with concrete.

Concrete bar

◀ The tops of the piles are joined with concrete bars. This is called a pile foundation.

Pile

Long strips of steel, called girders, are bolted to upright steel columns. This makes the frame. ▼

A trolley moves along this arm to move heavy loads.

Girder

Tower crane

Steel column

Safety strap

A tower crane can be built taller as the building gets higher.

Concrete

Steel bar

Concrete strengthened with steel is called reinforced concrete.

To make the floor, the builders ▲ bolt steel sheets to the girders. They lay steel bars over these to make a net. Finally, they pour concrete on top.

Steel sheet

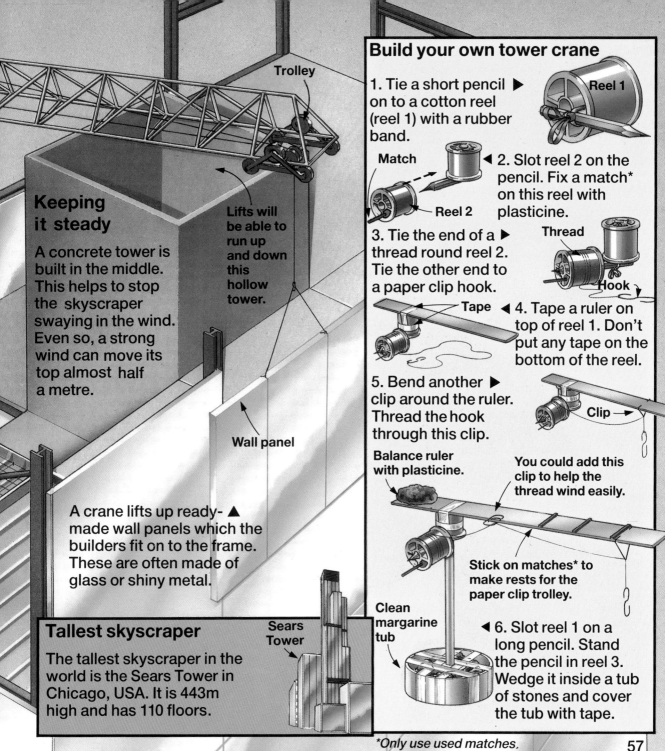

Trolley

Lifts will be able to run up and down this hollow tower.

Keeping it steady

A concrete tower is built in the middle. This helps to stop the skyscraper swaying in the wind. Even so, a strong wind can move its top almost half a metre.

Wall panel

A crane lifts up ready-made wall panels which the builders fit on to the frame. These are often made of glass or shiny metal.

Tallest skyscraper

The tallest skyscraper in the world is the Sears Tower in Chicago, USA. It is 443m high and has 110 floors.

Sears Tower

Build your own tower crane

1. Tie a short pencil ▶ on to a cotton reel (reel 1) with a rubber band.

Reel 1

2. Slot reel 2 on the ◀ pencil. Fix a match* on this reel with plasticine.

Match
Reel 2

3. Tie the end of a ▶ thread round reel 2. Tie the other end to a paper clip hook.

Thread
Hook

4. Tape a ruler on ◀ top of reel 1. Don't put any tape on the bottom of the reel.

Tape

5. Bend another ▶ clip around the ruler. Thread the hook through this clip.

Clip

Balance ruler with plasticine.

You could add this clip to help the thread wind easily.

Stick on matches* to make rests for the paper clip trolley.

Clean margarine tub

6. Slot reel 1 on a ◀ long pencil. Stand the pencil in reel 3. Wedge it inside a tub of stones and cover the tub with tape.

*Only use used matches.

57

Roads

Roads are made up of several layers. They need to be strong, because of all the cars and lorries which go over them every day.

Clearing the ground

1. First, the builders clear the ground. They cut down trees and use bulldozers to clear the bushes and stumps. ▶

◀ 2. Machines called scrapers and excavators dig out the bumps and fill in the hollows.

3. A large roller called a compactor is rolled over the ground to make it hard.

Roman roads

The Romans laid more than 80,000 kilometres of roads for soldiers to march over. Slaves had to carry earth and stones by hand to build up each layer. They put flat paving stones on top of their roads.

Bulldozer
These are called caterpillar treads. They grip bumpy ground.
These little metal feet stamp on the ground to make it firm.
Compactor
Scraper
Excavator
Blades scrape up the earth into this box.
This scoop can swing round to dump the earth.

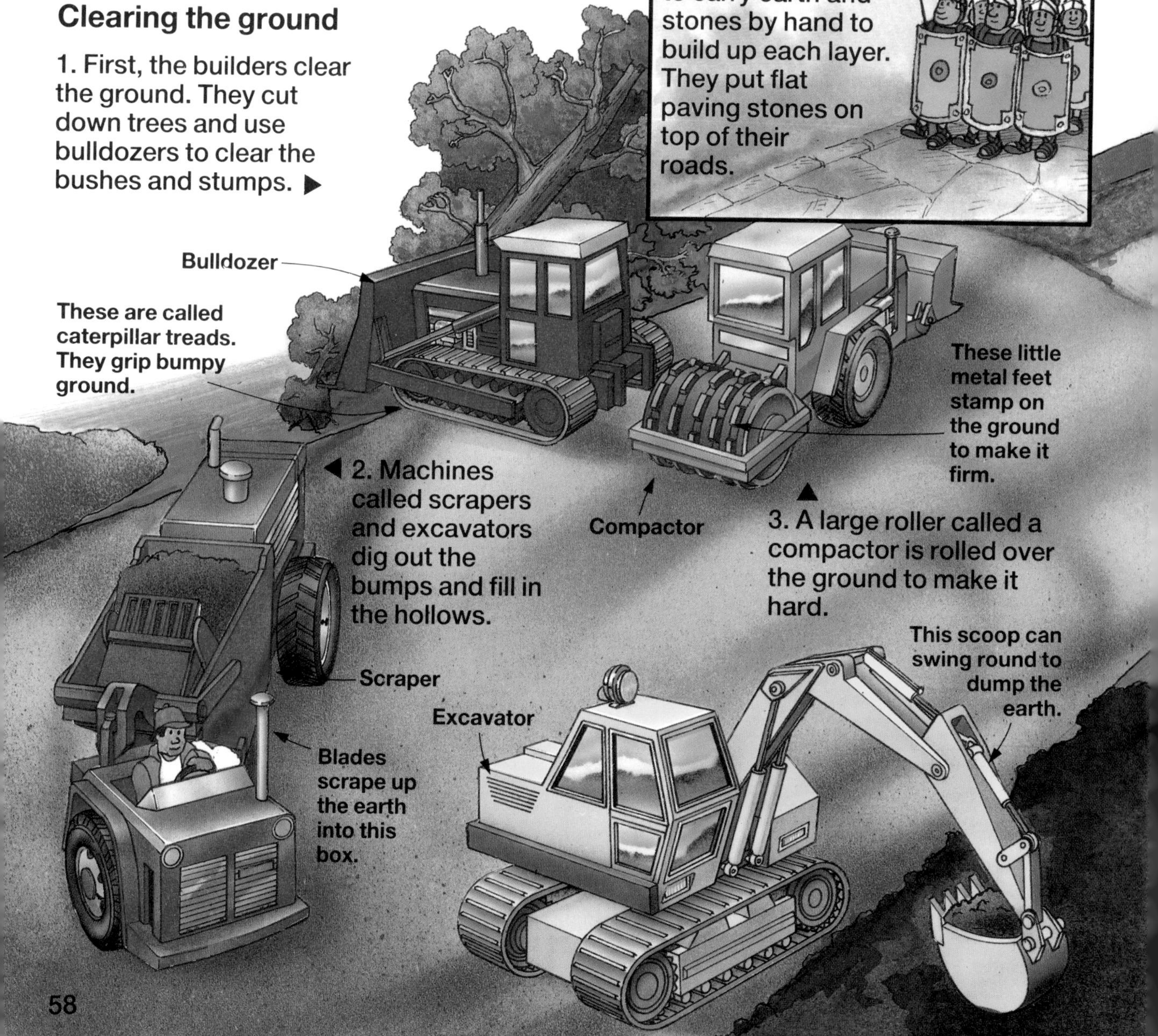

Starting to build

Crushed rock is spread over the soil. A machine called a grader levels this stony layer.

Grader

Flattening hills

Steep roads are difficult to drive on. Builders make a hill less steep by cutting out earth at the top and piling it up at the bottom.

Earth is piled up here.

Earth is cut out here.

Finishing it off

1. Hot asphalt (see page 70) is poured into the front of a machine called a paver. The paver spreads it evenly over the road.

Paver

Asphalt comes out here.

Asphalt is used because it is soft when hot and gets hard as it goes cold.

Road roller

Record roads

The USA has the most roads (over six million kilometres).

This length would go round the world 162 times.

The road roller has smooth metal rollers instead of wheels.

2. A heavy roller follows the paver. It presses the asphalt down, helping it to set hard.

3. Several layers of asphalt are put down. Stone chips are scattered on the top layer. These make the surface rough so car tyres will grip it safely.

59

Bridges

Bridges have to be very strong so that heavy lorries and trains can go across them.

On this page you can see how a bridge is built over a road.

1. First, concrete ledges (abutments) are built up on both sides of the road. Thick concrete walls (piers) are built in a line between them. ▼

Concrete is poured out here.

Abutment

Concrete pump

Steel rod

Beam

Crane

Pier

Pier

Concrete is tipped in here.

Pier

Abutment

▲
2. A crane lifts concrete beams on top of the piers and the abutments.

▲
3. The builders lay a criss-cross of steel rods on top of the beams. Concrete is pumped on top of the rods.

Brick arch bridges

Arches

Bridges used to be built by making arches out of brick. Builders joined lots of arches together to make long bridges.

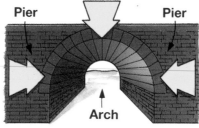

Pier

Pier

Arch

Brick arches are built between two thick brick piers. These stop the arch collapsing when weight is put on the bridge.

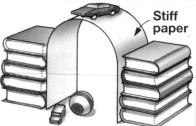

Stiff paper

Use two piles of books to keep a paper arch in place. The books will stop the arch from flattening even if you put a toy car on top.

Building over rivers

Building supports in a river is difficult and there are often wide gaps between them. Builders use several large concrete blocks to cross these gaps.

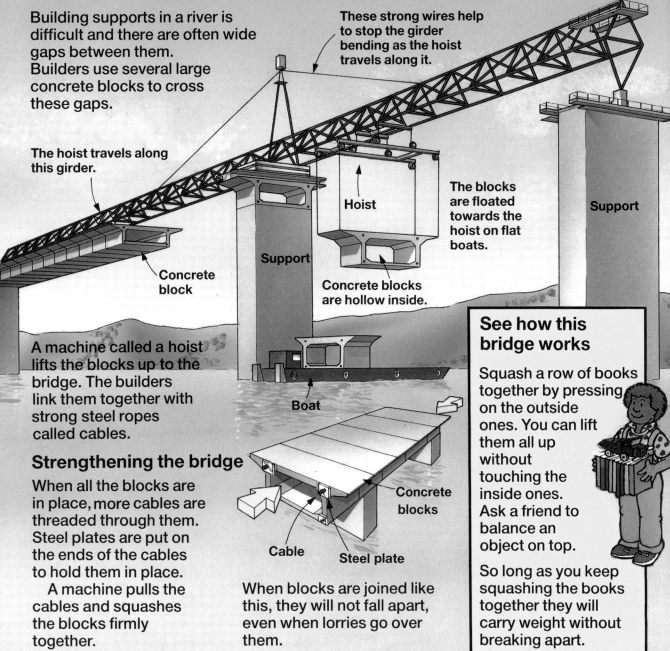

These strong wires help to stop the girder bending as the hoist travels along it.

The hoist travels along this girder.

Hoist

The blocks are floated towards the hoist on flat boats.

Support

Support

Concrete block

Concrete blocks are hollow inside.

Boat

A machine called a hoist lifts the blocks up to the bridge. The builders link them together with strong steel ropes called cables.

Strengthening the bridge

When all the blocks are in place, more cables are threaded through them. Steel plates are put on the ends of the cables to hold them in place.

A machine pulls the cables and squashes the blocks firmly together.

Concrete blocks

Cable

Steel plate

When blocks are joined like this, they will not fall apart, even when lorries go over them.

See how this bridge works

Squash a row of books together by pressing on the outside ones. You can lift them all up without touching the inside ones. Ask a friend to balance an object on top.

So long as you keep squashing the books together they will carry weight without breaking apart.

Suspension bridges

This is a suspension bridge. The road is hung (suspended) from two thick steel cables.

1. A concrete tower, ▶ shaped like a ladder, is built on either side of the river.

    The cables run across the tops of these towers. Their ends are fixed into lumps of concrete (anchorages) on the river banks.

Saddle

Tower

The cables go through metal grooves called saddles at the top of each tower.

Cable

One tower stands on each side of the river.

Anchorage

Steel deck

▲

2. A platform of steel (deck) stretches between the anchorages. The road is built on top of this.

Bottom rung

The anchorages have to be very strong to stop the cables being pulled out by the heavy road.

A famous suspension bridge

◀——— **Span** ———▶

The Humber Bridge has the longest span (distance between supports) of any bridge in the world. It measures 1,410m.

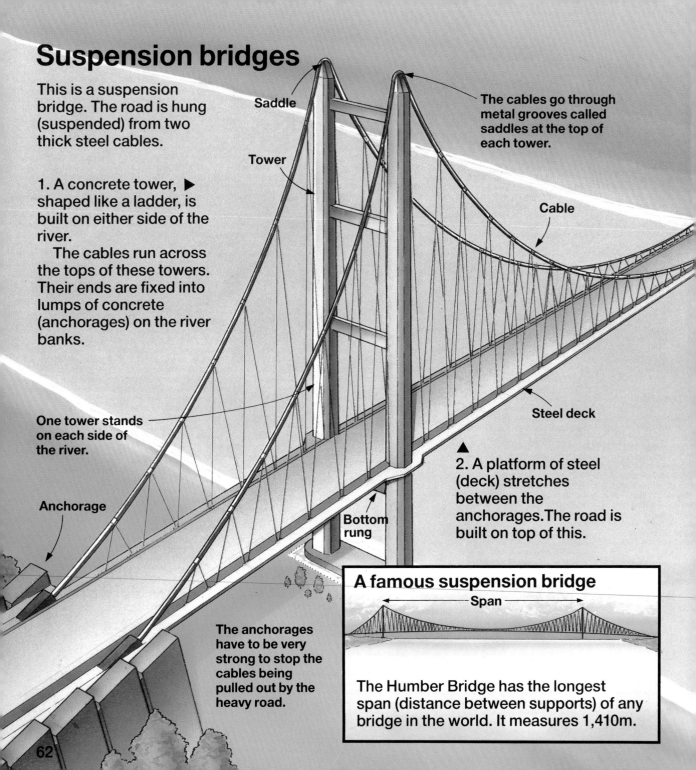

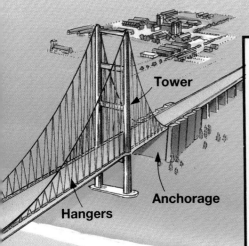

Tower

Anchorage

Hangers

Hangers

▲
3. Hangers join the deck on to the cables. These hold the road up so that it doesn't bend or break.

Getting the deck in place

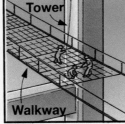

Tower

Walkway

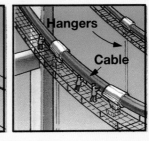

Hangers

Cable

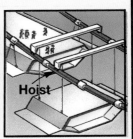

Hoist

1. Builders hang wire walkways between the towers. These are taken down when the bridge is finished.

2. They stand on the walkways to put the cables between the towers. They fix hangers to the cables.

3. A hoist lifts steel pieces up to the builders. They fix each piece to the hangers. This makes the deck.

Joining the deck together

When all the deck pieces are in place, some builders climb inside. They join pieces together with melted metal. This is called welding.
  Here is how they do it:

1. They put metal rods in the gaps between the pieces.

2. They use electric power to melt the rods.

3. The melted metal fills the gaps. It hardens as it cools.

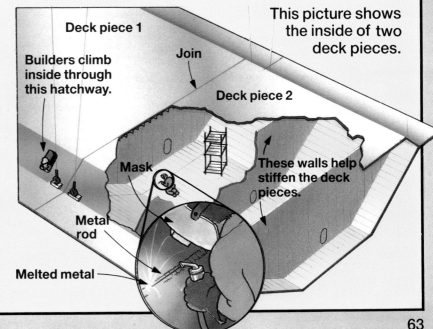

Deck piece 1

Builders climb inside through this hatchway.

Join

Deck piece 2

This picture shows the inside of two deck pieces.

Mask

These walls help stiffen the deck pieces.

Metal rod

Melted metal

63

Dams

Rivers overflow with water in winter but dry up in summer. Because of this, dams are built across rivers to store their water. A river blocked by a dam forms a huge lake called a reservoir.

Reservoir

Building the dam

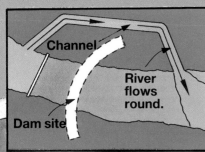

1. The builders blast underground channels through the valley's sides.

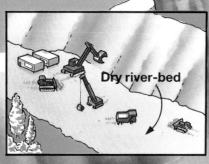

2. They use machines to dig out the river-bed until they reach a layer of solid rock.

This dam has a curved concrete wall. It is called an arch dam. It can hold back billions of tons of water.

Valley

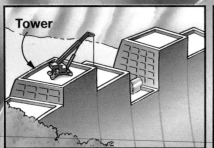

3. They now build several tall concrete towers on the layer of solid rock. They spray cement into the gaps between the towers to make one enormous dam wall.

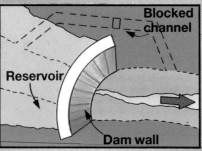

4. Finally, the underground channels are filled up with concrete. The river flows back until is blocked by the dam. A lot of water builds up to form the reservoir.

Power stations

When water flows fast it has a lot of power. This is turned into electricity in buildings called hydro-electric power stations.

These are built below dams where steep pipes can carry very fast-flowing water to them.

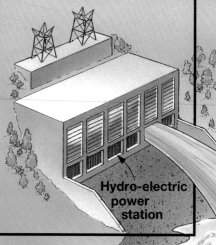

Hydro-electric power station

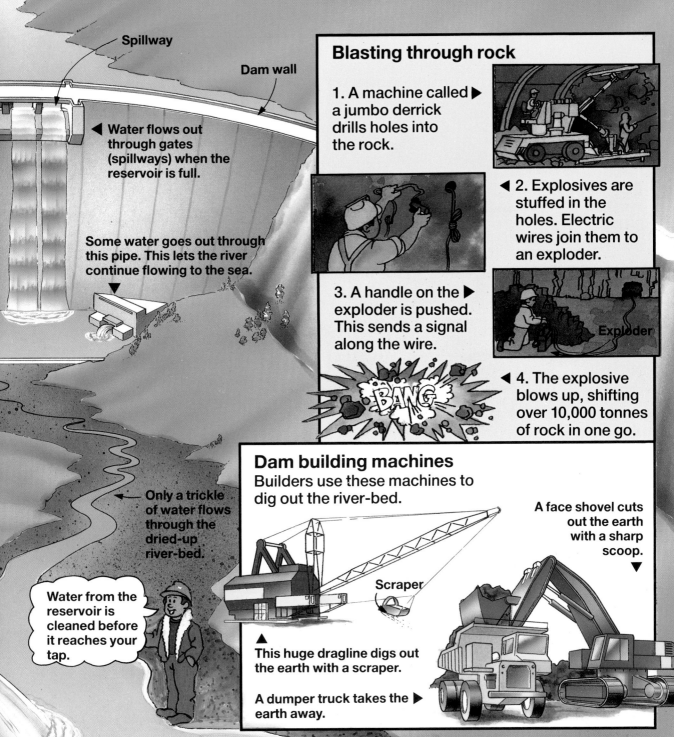

Spillway

Dam wall

◀ Water flows out through gates (spillways) when the reservoir is full.

Some water goes out through this pipe. This lets the river continue flowing to the sea.
▼

Only a trickle of water flows through the dried-up river-bed. ←

Water from the reservoir is cleaned before it reaches your tap.

Blasting through rock

1. A machine called ▶ a jumbo derrick drills holes into the rock.

◀ 2. Explosives are stuffed in the holes. Electric wires join them to an exploder.

3. A handle on the ▶ exploder is pushed. This sends a signal along the wire.

Exploder

BANG

◀ 4. The explosive blows up, shifting over 10,000 tonnes of rock in one go.

Dam building machines

Builders use these machines to dig out the river-bed.

A face shovel cuts out the earth with a sharp scoop.
▼

Scraper

▲
This huge dragline digs out the earth with a scraper.

A dumper truck takes the ▶ earth away.

Tunnels

Tunnels are built deep below cities, rivers, mountains and even the sea. Some are large enough for cars and trains to go through.

Large tunnels are made by this machine. It is called a TBM which stands for tunnel boring machine. It bores through the earth.

The earth falls off the conveyor belt here, into the trucks.

The conveyor belt takes the earth back along the tunnel.

When all the trucks are full they are taken away to be emptied.

Pieces of concrete go along rails to the lining arms.

Micro-tunnels

Tunnels for small pipes and drains are called micro-tunnels. Some micro-tunnels are dug by a machine called a remote-controlled drill. This is steered from a cabin on the ground above it.

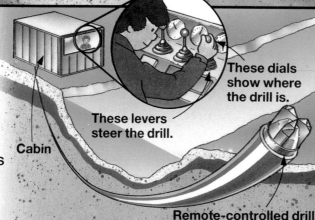

These dials show where the drill is.

These levers steer the drill.

Cabin

Remote-controlled drill

Dangerous tunnels

Freshly dug tunnels are often weak. Their sides could collapse, killing the builders. This TBM makes sure the tunnel does not collapse by lining the sides with concrete as it goes.

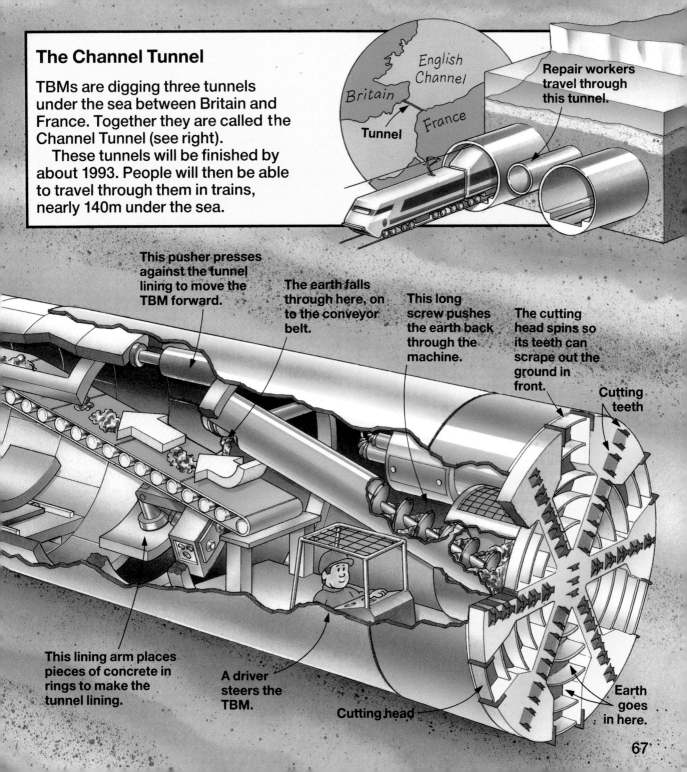

The Channel Tunnel

TBMs are digging three tunnels under the sea between Britain and France. Together they are called the Channel Tunnel (see right).

These tunnels will be finished by about 1993. People will then be able to travel through them in trains, nearly 140m under the sea.

English Channel

Britain

France

Tunnel

Repair workers travel through this tunnel.

This pusher presses against the tunnel lining to move the TBM forward.

The earth falls through here, on to the conveyor belt.

This long screw pushes the earth back through the machine.

The cutting head spins so its teeth can scrape out the ground in front.

Cutting teeth

This lining arm places pieces of concrete in rings to make the tunnel lining.

A driver steers the TBM.

Cutting head

Earth goes in here.

67

Offshore oil rigs

These rigs are drilling machines that get oil from under the sea. They are fixed to platforms which stand on the sea-bed. Over 100 people work on a platform. It must stand firm in rough seas to keep them safe.

Building the platform

Gates keep out the sea.

1. Workers build the platform at a place near the sea called a dry dock.

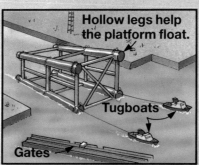

Hollow legs help the platform float.

Tugboats

Gates

2. Builders open the gates to let water into the dock. The platform is towed out to sea.

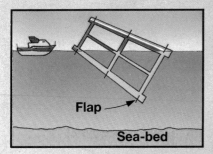

Flap

Sea-bed

3. Builders open flaps in the legs to let water in. The platform sinks and stands upright on the sea-bed.

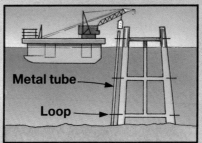

Metal tube

Loop

4. Tubes are hammered through loops on each leg. These go deep into the sea-bed to keep the platform in place.

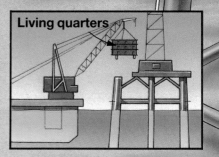

Living quarters

5. Boats carry out the rig and living quarters. A floating crane lifts them up on top of the platform.

Helideck

Helicopters land here to take people on and off the rig.

Living quarters are high above the waves.

Workers live here for two or three weeks at a time.

Platform

The platform rests on these long legs.

The legs are often more than 200m long.

Waste gas from the oil is burned here.

This crane is fixed to the platform. It lifts supplies off ships.

Diver's living chamber

Rig

Diving bell

Building underwater

Divers work underwater to check and mend parts of the oil rig and its platform.

They breathe air which goes down to them through a thick tube. They carry emergency air tanks in case this tube breaks.

This breathing tube is called an umbilical.

Emergency air tank

Waves often damage oil rigs. The divers look for cracks and rust. They repair any damage they find by ways such as welding (see page 63).

Moon pool

Lifeboat

This diving bell goes down through a hole called a moon pool. It takes divers to work under the sea.

Waves up to 30 metres high crash against the sides of the platform.

The oil rushes up to the surface through this pipe.

69

What buildings are made of

Egyptians probably used cement in their pyramids.

	Name	Where it comes from	What it is used for
	Asphalt. Black, stony mixture.	It is made by mixing crushed rock with hot bitumen.	It is spread on roads to make a tough surface (page 59).
	Bitumen. Thick, sticky oil.	Sometimes it seeps out of the ground. Sometimes it is drilled out by oil rigs.	It is mixed with crushed rock to make asphalt for roads.
	Bitumenised felt. Black, waterproof material.	It is made by spreading bitumen on rough felt.	It is used to stop damp rising up walls (page 53).
	Brick. A hard block of clay.	Clay is shaped into bricks. These are put into a kiln (see page 30) to harden them.	Bricks are used for building walls (page 53). Bricklayers stick them together with mortar.
	Cement. Fine powder.	It is made from clay and chalk. These are mixed, burnt and then ground up.	It sticks sand and stones together. It is used in concrete and mortar.
	Concrete. A type of man-made rock.	It is made by mixing sand, broken stones, cement and water. It sets hard when dry.	Concrete is used to make lots of things such as blocks, towers, columns and foundations.

The fastest bricklayer in the world is Ralph Charnock of Great Britain. He once laid 725 bricks in an hour.

Thousands of years ago, builders used bitumen to stick bricks together instead of mortar.

The tallest building in the world, the Warsaw Radio Mast, is made of steel. It is 646m tall.

	Name	Where it comes from	What it is used for
	Mortar. Gritty paste which dries hard.	It is made by mixing sand, cement and water.	It is used to stick bricks together (page 53).
	Plaster. Stiff paste which is hard and smooth when dry.	A rock called gypsum is ground to a fine powder and then mixed with sand and water.	It is spread over brick and concrete walls to make them smooth (page 55).
	Plasterboard. Stiff board.	It is made by sandwiching plaster between two sheets of paper.	It is used to make ceilings and some inside walls (page 54).
	Reinforced concrete. Very strong concrete.	It is made by letting concrete set around steel rods or bars.	It is often used to make bridges because it is so strong cars and lorries can go over it (page 60).
	Steel. Very strong metal.	It is made from iron which has been heated in a furnace (see pages 40-41).	Pieces of steel are joined together to make things such as bridges, oil rigs and skyscrapers.
	Wood. The inside of a tree.	Trees are cut down and sawn up to make pieces of wood for building.	It is used to make floors and roof frames in many houses. Some houses are made just from wood.

Did you know that the largest concrete building in the world is the Grand Coulee Dam?

It is on the Columbia River, USA.

Building records

★The oldest buildings in the world are 21 huts in France. They were built about 400,000 years ago.

★The largest building in the world is in Holland. The floor covers 368, 477m or 50 football pitches.

Houses

★The largest house is in North Carolina, USA. It has 250 rooms and a garden as big as 6,644 football pitches.

★A cottage in Wales has only two tiny rooms and a staircase. The whole house is 1.8m wide and 3m high.

Skyscrapers

★The first skyscraper ever was the Home Insurance Building in Chicago, USA. It was 52m high and was built in 1885.

★The top six tallest skyscrapers are:

Sears Tower, Chicago USA	443m
World Trade Centre, New York, USA	411m
Empire State Building, New York, USA	381m
Standard Oil Building, Chicago, USA	346m
John Hancock Centre, Chicago, USA	343m
Chrysler Building, New York, USA	319m

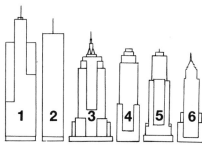

Nearly 17,000 people work in the Sears Tower – the population of a small town. It has 103 lifts, and 16,000 windows.

Roads

★The countries with the most roads are:

USA	6,365,590km
Canada	3,002,000km
France	1,502,000km
Brazil	1,411,936km
USSR	1,408,800km

★The busiest road in the world is in Los Angeles, California, USA. About 363 vehicles per minute travel along it.

Bridges

★The oldest suspension bridge (see page 62) that still exists was built in 1470. It is in Yunnan Province, China.

★A bridge in Japan that joins Honshu and Shikoku islands is 3560m long.

Tunnels

★The longest tunnel is the New York City West Delaware water supply tunnel. It is 168.9km long.

★London has 408km of underground train tunnels which carry 800 million passengers a year.

Dams and oil rigs

★The highest dam is the Nurek Dam (USSR). It is 300m high – only 50cm shorter than the Eiffel Tower in Paris.

★The tallest oil rig is the BP Magnus in the North Sea. It is 312m tall.

Index

Answers

Page 5 – Pitta, chapattis, soda and naan are all unleavened.

Page 43 – Polyamide, Lycra, aramid, elastane, polypropylene, Terylene, Crimplene and acetate are some other synthetic and man-made fibres.

Page 48 – 135 million sheep.

LEGO® is a registered trade mark belonging to the LEGO group and is used here by special permission.

Acknowledgements

We wish to thank the following people and organisations for their help:

Transmanche Link, Gifford and Partners, Col. W. I. F. Austin, Jonathan Louth B.A. (Hons)Arch, Dip.Arch., Wharton Williams and Comex Houlder Limited.

First published in 1989 by
Usborne Publishing Ltd
Usborne House
83-85 Saffron Hill
London EC1N 8RT.

Printed in Belgium